Total-E-Bound Publishing books by Alcamia Payne:

Chickadee

I0570746

SINFUL TREASURE

ALCAMIA PAYNE

Sinful Treasure
ISBN # 978-1-78184-563-9
©Copyright Alcamia Payne 2013
Cover Art by Posh Gosh ©Copyright September 2012
Interior text design by Claire Siemaszkiewicz
Total-E-Bound Publishing

Published in 2013 by Total-E-Bound Publishing, Think Tank, Ruston Way, Lincoln, LN6 7FL, United Kingdom.

SINFUL
TREASURE

Dedication

Thanks as always to Z, you know who you are!

Prologue

Pandora's Box of sinful treasure was brought to her carried aloft on the shoulders of the God Mercury. In my case, the sinful box came to me in the arms of my lover and it was a more dangerous box than Pandora's could ever have been. At least there was still hope left in the bottom of her casket whereas, my sinister inheritance was a mischief-making Loki, a jinni demon, Lord Bem — a lord of smouldering desire who was to be my salvation, my passion and my lover.

When I'd first seen the casket, I'd been torn between fear and loathing. It was as ancient as time and heavily engraved with symbols — entwined branches and serpents, from between which peeped ugly little monkey faces, signalling the mischief locked within, and daring the wary not to unlock it.

Left this deadly inheritance, at first I'd felt compelled to sit and study it in the evenings in the dark light from the lamp, and during the day I covered it from prying eyes with a black cloth. Shankar had told me many tales about it and, I knew I ought to dispose of it before this despicable tool of enchantment wove the same magic spell around me that it had indelibly woven around my lover Shankar.

On more than one occasion I had tried to destroy it when the box still only held the insubstantial consciousness of Bem and not, as it did later on, that beautiful pure thing I so sinfully stole – the soul of my one true love.

Once, I took it down to the pool at the bottom of the garden and, thinking it was heavy and it would sink in the holy waters from the mountain, I swam out with it and tried to submerge it. But the box caught in the eddies from the waterfall and simply turning in dizzying circles, bobbed towards me, caressing my arm, my leg, as if even then Bem's spirit was reminding me, 'Soon you'll belong to me, Emma'. Touching the keys around my neck and still thinking of consigning the dark denizen to oblivion, I let them slip from my fingers hoping to lose them in the depths, thus sealing his fate as a prisoner forever in the casket. But an invisible hand seemed to catch them, arresting their progress and making them catch on the tangled stem of a lotus where their black pearl inlay glittered in the shafts of light. It was like being followed by a legion of little goblins because I never seemed able to rid myself of Bem's presence, and every time I tried to dispose of the keys, they were artfully returned.

I also tried burying Pandora's Box of sin deep in the cleansing earth, but the next morning when I woke up, I discovered that overnight the rains had come, and when I looked under the dancing fronds of the giant palm where I'd dug the hole – a very deep hole it might be said – it had somehow popped up, tilted at an angle. As Vasi would say, "It isn't that easy to rid yourself of destiny, especially a passionate destiny."

Chapter One

Part One

The Present

I had to pin up my hair, I thought, and do what all women did to make themselves attractive. Standing in my bedroom in front of the mirror, I was suddenly struck by a thought. *Who was this stunning changed woman backlit by the lamp and surrounded in a supernatural nimbus of light?* Of course it was me, but for a moment I didn't recognise myself. *Come along, Emma, you must force yourself to put on this gorgeous dress and walk out of Langhousa, just to prove there's another world – a mortal world beyond these walls – and you're still a part of it. Come on, you must.* Touching my throat, I fought the feeling now descending over me in an invisible veil. It was very difficult fighting these forces, especially when I didn't want to. By this time I realised Bem's passion had taken me over and he'd bent and twisted my world into shapes of such dark desire I couldn't break free – and did I really want to? I was partly to blame. You see, I Emma Spence, had committed a terrible sin. My wish had somehow come true and I loved a demon from another world, a demon called Bem who clothed himself in the flesh and blood of my dead lover.

"Yes, that's it, Emma," I chided, sliding a comb into my thick hair. "One step at a time and don't think too far ahead." Although it was hard not to, when I knew for a certainty David was planning on asking me to marry him again tonight. He'd always intended to. About nine months ago my suspicions had been confirmed when I'd overheard him talking about it to Lucas Fairweather at Granny's ninety-eighth birthday party. I had slipped out onto the veranda to enjoy the cool night air for a moment and the two of them had been standing by the buffet table.

"Emma cuts a striking picture, doesn't she," Lucas had commented. "She's the most beautiful woman for miles around."

"Yes, and you know I intend to marry her one day?" David had retorted.

My heart had been beating a rapid tattoo and I'd been filled with an odd mixture of emotions as I'd strained to hear above the chatter of voices.

"God, are you crazy? All of the Spence women are touched." Lucas, his best friend, had chortled.

"Touched? Oh, come on," David had continued persuasively. "She's simply different—she's entitled to be, that's what makes her an angel and so utterly fascinating. How many angels do you know?"

I smiled. Of course, I was different, at least David had got that right. The fact he appreciated I had more to me than most of the young women in Chandrapoor made me inclined to feel warmly towards him. David was always standing up for me and fighting my corner.

"She's different, granted, but hardly an angel." Lucas had elaborated. "The entire family are touched by the devil. I recall some exceedingly strange tales, tales to do with dabbling, you know? Why, the old woman's a veritable entertainment piece. She's into witchcraft and mediumship, not to mention that palaver of reading tea leaves and cards and seeing ghosts. My God, man, it wouldn't be that other fascinating thing — the sex thing, that draws you to the girl, now would it?" At this point he'd clapped David on the back. "I can't say I blame you in that respect. Rowena Spence is how old? Ninety-eight? And by all accounts she's still feisty in bed and has that way of inciting and sashaying her behind like a whore. But Emma!" He had been turning his cigar around and around in his fingers. "She's far crazier than the old lady and quite insane, walking about in a trance most of the time and talking to those fairies and spirits and suchlike. I wouldn't blame you, though, old man. She's stinking rich and perhaps you fancy a challenge."

For just an instant my heart sank, but Lucas was right and why should I deny it? The Spence's were different and I was glad that we were. Lucas annoyed me, though. I hated to be thought of as a rich heiress, hunted down because I was both attractive and the recipient of a small fortune. My heart had been in my mouth waiting for David's reply.

"Good Lord, it's not about the money." David had paused. "And, it's most definitely not about the sex. I find her lovely, stunning and charming and quite, how do they say, fey and whimsical?"

Once, he had pushed me into the corner next to the piano in Laura Godsey's parlour. "Kiss me, Emma, I want to see."

"See what?" I'd attempted to force him away. "What do you want to see? If I'm capable of kissing you, or if like a vampire I'll suck your blood? Have you been having bets on me? Is that it David?" I'd been fuming when I had pushed him back with my hand. "What do you say in secret to Lucas, that you want to fuck me and see if I'm a virgin?"

I think he liked my flaring personality and the anger that rose so easily to the surface, but on this occasion I had been easily quenched. He'd pushed me back, his expression one of being wounded. "Oh no," he had said. "None of that. They speculate about you, everyone does, but I don't care a jot. You're extraordinary and I love you, Emma." He'd been soft and persuasive as his hand cradled my breast. "Don't be defensive and nasty. You're just so ethereal and pure looking I want to see if you're really like that. I don't believe in all that airy fairy stuff I truly don't, but when I kiss you a part of me feels compelled to believe it. I want to see if you're enchanted like they say you are and if you'll enchant me...if these lips" — he touched them gently with his finger — "feel as soft on me as I think they will."

"Don't be silly." I turned my face away.

Undeniably David was good-looking. He had a pleasant round Nordic face with wavy blond hair and blue eyes. I think I was fond of him because he wasn't a dynamic sex threat like most men and he wasn't the type to put his hand on your breast or cunt. No, he was the kind of man who'd respond well to a domineering woman and something about that excited me. Especially when I imagined him naked and hands bound, crouching at my bed post whilst I whipped him. My escapism into fantasy was one of my small indulgences and I allowed myself it, because it gave me pleasure and pleasure was hard to come by. Anyway, if the whispers were true, I was insane so what was the harm? I was hardly going to actually gratify these daydreams was I?

Sitting naked in front of my dressing table, I leant forward, peering at myself critically stroking a little rouge over my cheeks and attempting to drag my thoughts back to the present. "Well, dear, this will never do," I muttered, tracing my thumb under my eye. I'd become increasingly pale recently and I doubted that any amount of powder or rouge would hide the dark shadows. I'd always been very pale, and as Granny used to say 'a true English Rose', but now my pallor had translated into an ethereal and haunting kind of beauty—the beauty coming from being touched by the finger of darkness, and that rendered me a mortal walking in two worlds.

Bem was there in the corner, his smouldering dark gaze whispering over my skin.

"Why, are you doing this, why do you insist on this plan?" he said in his melodious, seductive lilt. "Is this the way you try to punish me, Emma, or are you trying to rehabilitate your soul before it's too late?" He stepped forward his angular features cast into relief by the glow from the lamp. "You were so casual about the mortal you, so ready to release it, and now you seem to try and cling to it in desperation, like it's a life raft or something."

"You have such a lovely way with words," I replied, pouting at the mirror and unscrewing my lipstick to dot the colour on my lips. "And perhaps you're right because I feel that the tether holding me to mortal is exceptionally fragile indeed." I stroked my mother's double strand of black pearls, holding them up to my neck and tossing back my blonde hair.

I was finding it distressing having to think about David, but it was impossible to turn down his invitation, especially on my birthday. I had to attend the odd dinner party or shopping trip, but it was becoming increasingly harder every time. I sprayed my body in light rose eau de cologne—under my arms, behind my ears and inside my cunt as if I anticipated a man was going to thrust his nose or mouth inside me. I could tell that it annoyed Bem, whose eyebrows knitted together in a frown.

"You were made to be a mortal whore," he observed a little nastily, stepping into the lamp's full glare, his dark eyes flashing. "Do you want me to put your pearls on for you angel?"

"No thank you." He reached out his hand and I moved away. I knew that a finger on my skin would be enough to weave the spell, enough to melt me. Instead, I fastened the pearls myself, and when I moved the chair back, the sight of my naked body in the mirror with just the black pearl necklace was enough to arouse even me.

I raised my foot on the bed and smoothed my thighs with my fingers, aware he was staring at the tuft of my sex. He licked his lips and crept forward with the stealth of a panther, his eyes half closed in lascivious contemplation of that place. He'd come and do it now if I wanted him to, and the thought of it gave me a strange feeling of power. He would kneel there in front of me, and holding my buttocks, bring me to melting orgasm with his demon tongue. I shivered, rolling my stockings up my legs then clipping them in place—his smouldering gaze following my every movement.

"I thought you'd dispensed with all that gaudy finery, the stockings and the garters, the things that imprison your womanhood. You could at least have let me dress you. I would have felt better knowing my hands had been there before his. Then tonight when he touches you, you'd feel me consuming you, evaporating that mortal contact. You will let him caress you, won't you, you're bound to? How can you not let him? I curse him and I'll keep cursing him until he melts away." Bem was pacing, his handsome head bowed, his long raven black hair flopping forward. "You'll let him put that morbid mortal taint on you again, won't you? So, when you get back, I'll have to carry you to the bath and bathe you all over, inside and out just to rid us both of it." He made a face. "Ugh, it's rank, that taste of mortal man, worse than curdled milk. It makes me sick to think of it."

I could have dignified this with a response. Instead, I stared a reprimand at him in the mirror. He was making me shiver, his strong psychic powers trying to connect with me as they danced through the air like ripples across a celestial pond. The light scintillating off his thick hair, he sprawled sexily in the chair by the fireplace, staring at me with his chin on his fist and his legs apart. "We'll sort it out later though, darling. I won't upset you before you go. I don't want to spoil your birthday, and of course, if you feel you want to prove something to yourself you must do it. You must come to me without a shadow of a doubt, without fearing mental bondage or any such ridiculous thing."

"It's not a case of having to prove anything." Walking over to the bed, I shook out my gown, the glorious ivory silk catching the light and spinning rainbows. "I'm simply clinging to human since I'm still alive, still flesh and blood. But, you can see, can't you, that it's becoming harder to cling to the familiar things? Even simple things like eating and brushing my hair have become difficult. The purpose of tonight is"—I paused—"to see if I can still participate in life, because if I can't you know what will happen, don't you? Some fool like Mrs Fassbender or even Marylyn—since now even Marylyn shuns me—will send for a doctor at that insane institute and they'll have me locked up. They're like vultures, Bem. I'm sure they want to take Langhousa off me." I nervously rolled the pearls between my fingers.

His mouth twisted in a cruel smile. "I don't see how they can do anything. That's why you go to see Mr Panjari in Delhi, isn't it? He's tied up your will and fastened any loopholes with his considerable legal skill."

"Tonight's about principles. Don't you see?" My face folded into what I imagined was a sorrowful mask and I could feel tears pushing at the backs of my eyes. "I'm confused and I never thought I'd say it, but I think I want your dirty dark world. The trouble is though, Bem, I'm tethered to this life and there are some things I still like about mortality. Books, for instance, and the feel of life and yes, those silly banal female things like shopping and coffee and, well..." I tugged a comb through my thick hair before twisting it up and digging the pins in with sharp angry jabs. "Just being human, being in flesh. You said so yourself that you adored flesh. That even in the guise of a demon you thrilled at the feel of a corporeal overcoat in which to flaunt your alien beauty, an overcoat, I may add, I so kindly furnished you with."

He steepled his fingers under his chin, and his gaze was as deep and fathomless as a pool. "God, you're so fast in an argument, so cutting in a riposte. I'd never let those vultures take Langhousa off you, you know that, don't you?"

"You'd have no choice if the doctor said I was crazy and talking to demons and they bundled me in that van. So, you see why I must do these things?"

Bem jumped to his feet, placing his hands on my shoulders. "Yes, Emma, regrettably I do. Let me attend to this, let me zip it up." He took the dress off me, his hand sliding onto my butt and separating the crack so he could place his finger there while I stepped inside the sumptuous fabric. He inched the dress up and fastened the tiny buttons his fingers burning like liquid fire on my spine, before kissing my neck with definite, firm kisses like punctuation marks, he gazed over my shoulder at me in the glass.

I gave him a look of mute appeal.

"Do you remember how we used to do this? I washed and dressed you and sprayed your eau de cologne and dusted talc between your legs. I could have done it tonight. I could have knelt at your feet and been your slave." Bem moaned.

"Whose slave is whose? I don't wish to feel your ownership tonight." I shimmied, and the tiny glass beads attached to sleeve and hem like trapped teardrops, shone in the light.

"Ownership—that sour point." He was stroking his chin.

"Oh please." I turned around. "Don't be like this. You know I have to prove to myself that my world exists. You've found your paradise." Sitting down I picked up my slippers and slid one on. He was there immediately, taking them off me and stroking my stockings.

"No, let me do that. Do you recollect how I did this once before, on that day I saved you, Emma? You'd gone to the market to buy saffron and that man chased you up the alley. You broke your heel and I had to come and save you." His smile broadened. "You were confused, because even then I was painting you with my world. Yes, even then I had your lover in my hand and he was turning to me and it was Bem Hazari—demon lord—and not Shankar—feeble mortal—who held the strings of your destiny. How could it be otherwise when I'd mesmerised his human soul? And you knew it the moment you laid eyes on him, you felt that fatal attraction and you wanted it. You always did. Is it any wonder he was charmed by a creature like you, something uniquely appetising to mortal and demon, a creature that since her mortal birth had been morphing into something glorious?" He peered up at me, his eyes full of silent entreaty. "On that day you were a butterfly coming out of its cocoon, flexing its womanly and otherworld power and glowing with promise. If it's possible for a woman to become more beautiful day by day you were she."

I turned away from his piercing gaze, gripping the arms of the chair. I could recall that day so well. A man had followed me up a side street. He'd appeared from nowhere, a fleet panther. He'd pushed up against me, a white man, someone I took to be a businessman. Pinning me between the wall and his body and brutally pushing aside my underwear, he'd stuck his finger so roughly up inside my sex that it had brought tears to my eyes. I'd raised my knee and kicked him in the groin the way Granny had taught me, before I'd fled sobbing up a dirty side street where the gutters had been overflowed with filth and stray dogs had sniffed at my feet. I'd tucked myself into the dark shadows of a doorway, heart hammering. At first I'd thought he'd followed me because, when I had looked up, I had seen a man in a rather crumpled white linen suit staring down at me with molten eyes of such inexpressible emotion my head had swum and I had had to steady myself. It was Shankar – the man I'd come to love with all my heart.

Men followed me everywhere. It was part of the curse of being a Spence woman that I couldn't shake off. I wasn't a whore and I was sure I did nothing to invite it, but as Granny Rowena used to say, 'A Spence woman is a Spence woman and she has a sex magic about her that attracts men like bees around a honeypot'.

"Men can be such beasts and I'm a man, of course. You trust me don't you?" He'd grinned at me. "I'm a doctor so let me see that foot. You went down hard and I think you twisted it."

Yes, I'd thought with a moan of consternation, glancing down, and seeing I'd broken the heel on my shoe. My foot really did hurt.

Crouching down, he'd unfastened the strap inspecting the broken heel of the shoe carefully, then, holding my foot and putting it on his knee, he had spent a great deal of time manipulating it. For the first time in my life I'd yielded to one orgasm after another, precipitated solely by the touch of his fingers.

"It's only bruised. Lean on me and I'll take you back to the hotel."

We'd crossed the market square. No one had seemed to notice I was walking in my stockinged feet, the doctor holding my shoes in one hand and my arm in the other, his hand on my flesh burning every place he'd touched. In the hotel foyer he'd done something unthinkable for an Indian gentleman. Before I had time to complain, he'd scooped me up and carried me to my room. Once there, he'd unlocked the door, ferried me to the bed and, unclipping my suspender belt and rolling my stockings down my leg, he had begun bending my ankle this way and that to test for an injury. I'd wanted him to kiss it and yes, then he had been kissing it all over as strange shivers pulsed through me and his eyes teased me.

"After today, you shouldn't walk through the market alone. I don't know how to say this without offending you, but you're one of those women, the type of woman who'll always attract attention. It's not just that hair, although that's enough to catch any man's eye…and it's not your unusual beauty. It's the sex, my dear, you exude it. You're blatantly sex. If you were my wife I'd have you in a veil, I'd cover every inch of you."

Shankar's finger had trickled down my face, circling my lips and stroking back my hair that had fallen free from its pins. Then, standing up he'd fetched a bowl and had begun carefully washing my feet. He'd been so tender, so beguiling. But he'd been human then.

"Now," I said sourly. "In case you were wondering, I didn't encourage that horrible man's attention."

"No, my sweet, you didn't. You can't help having something like an extra finger or toe, something that makes people stare. You were born with it."

"Yes, born with it," I muttered quietly. "You're right, I invite sex."

* * * *

And, I did invite sex, I knew that I did, I pondered, snapped once more back to the present.

I'd had to face facts early on in my life. I was not like other women, I never had been. I travelled between worlds and I craved things a mortal man couldn't give me—bliss, an ecstatic union that had its birth and completion in the fiery metamorphosis of spiritual love. Like a firefly I moved through life inviting, touching and caressing and encouraging constant attention and sometimes assault. I could have married a diplomat or a prince and yet being fey, a woman of spirit with this craving for sex burning in me—mortal man could never assuage my thirsts—not even a king would do.

Bem fed me what I knew I needed and couldn't live without. A poisonous cocktail of sex and desire. It made me, Emma Spence, a slave to mysterious visions of the other world and it lured me with powerful sex feelings. Every day I was seeing and feeling more as the torrid Kundalini serpent unwound his coils of passion in my belly. What would Granny think of me now? I peered in the mirror and the possessed Emma Spence peered back with her vacant, cobalt-blue eyes. Rowena had always told me that I was the most alluring and wicked of the Spence women, and she'd been right.

I put my hand on Bem's cheek, my heart welling up. He was a cruel facsimile of my lover and it was hard to perceive the devilish core lurking beneath the magical fabric of fake skin and bone. All I could see was the reflection of Shankar. He teased me, tracing my thumb around his mouth with his own and I pressed my lips against his, delighting in the flicker of his tongue.

"A demon I might be," he whispered. "Nevertheless, I'm eaten up by the way men stare and lust for you."

"Darling," I replied. "Darling, I don't mean for it to be like this. I do belong to you, truly I do."

Chapter Two

Granny Rowena raised me after Mother had died and I'd grown up on the Langhousa plantation, being fed an endless diet of spiritual trivia. Granny had told me that the Spence line was very special indeed and it was the lot of the Spence women to be tarnished to a greater or lesser degree with an indelible stain — the thing my great-grandmother had called far seeing. All of the Spences had been touched by it, right back to the fourteenth-century when Wilberta Spence, a woman of indeterminate blood and an exotic kind of gypsy witch from faraway shores, had been taken prisoner by Jeremiah Spence. Jeremiah had been intoxicated with Wilberta's extraordinary beauty and he'd brought her back to England to be his wife.

Wilberta had made no secret of the fact that she spoke to spirits, and often she'd entertain them in courtly parlance in the large dining room at Spence Place back in Richmond, Surrey. Here the table would be laid with the Spence finery and the invited guests in doublet and hose and assorted historical paraphernalia would sit and entertain her. Jeremiah, her husband and guest of honour had been invited and apparently he'd been so besotted with his new wife that he indulged her macabre games of charades while she'd laughed and chattered to the invisible chairs.

This weirdness, this compulsion to step across a thin veil to the other side of spirit was a disease of the Spences and the Spence women preserved some strange ideas to do with that world. For instance, Rowena had told me that human birth was a funny thing and only one tiny part of a larger puzzle. She'd said there were guardians on the other side and when a human body was born into this mortal world and the mortal cord was snipped by the doctor, occasionally, and for some reason, the spiritual guardians chose not to detach the spiritual umbilical cord uniting mortal to spirit. Whatever reason they had to maintain contact with the Spence women, Rowena had said that we ought to feel flattered they'd chosen to intervene and direct our affairs like distant staunch family members, but that I could expect from time to time to feel a tug on that umbilical cord. It meant I was destined to live and love within two worlds, mortal and spirit, a challenge she pointed out, because many folk were driven insane by such a conundrum.

As if that wasn't enough—us poor Spences also carried another burden.

The spiritual stain caused much idle speculation and amusement among the Chandrapoor set—that flock of gossiping, straitlaced women—and was only excused due to the Spence women's other hefty weight of mental responsibility, our seductive beauty, charm and sexuality. This sexuality and the considerable Spence wealth that went with it, were blessings in some respects since they allowed a certain leniency where shortcomings were concerned. Thus we were embellished by a sensual mercurial charm, or bluntly put, a healthy liking for sex—this disease of sex having various implications, notably making us compelling women and irresistible enigmas to men.

We were at one and the same time chaste, obsessive and sufferers of a terrible mortal burden, notably lack of contentment, none of us able to find a shred of fulfilment with mortal man. It seemed that all of us were held in a vacuum of suspense, trapped on the one hand between the world of spirit, burden enough it seemed, and on the other the victims of idolatrous sex worship. The Spence women believed that sex transcended the physical body and they looked for more than a quick frolic under the bed sheets. In fact, they were obsessed with finding the orgasmic Holy Grail. Mortal man didn't satisfy the yearnings we had for richer, deeper and more dangerous erotic liaisons, which gave us our legendary sexual thirst.

Of course, it was looked upon as somewhat quaint to be so daringly different but it was a curse. Caught on an endless wheel of fate, it seemed our lot to be disappointed in mortal love and to forever be lost souls, cast adrift and seeking something we knew existed but we couldn't properly see. It was similar to picking out the indistinct features of a blurry photograph.

I learnt about that dark stain of sexuality early on. Wherever I went, men had gazed at me with lust-filled intent, not quite identifying what quality I had. I didn't consider myself in the least bit pretty, although Granny said I was. In my view, my long fair hair gave me an insipid appearance and my eyes being dark like

Granny's, stood out and dominated my heart-shaped face.

"You're striking, Emma, but you realise that," she'd said. "Such beauty will unfortunately attract more than its fair share of adulation from men." At this point she'd paused and a dark curtain had seemed to drop over her face. "And, darling, be warned, it might also draw the attentions of other darker spectres." She'd stared at me unflinchingly with eyes that were exceptionally blue and separated by startling black rings

"What demons?" I'd asked. "You mean I could have a demon lover? Granny, how thrilling."

Granny shook her head. She'd been incredibly serious. "You mustn't joke about it, Emma, it's so easy to be tempted, it really is. You only have to think of Serena."

We'd been having tea in Granny's large conservatory, that was more like a splendid hot house, full to brimming with exotic plants. She'd insisted on having one built similar to her own mother's back home in England, where she could indulge her penchant for fabulous orchids and also other flowers. The boughs of the tree above my head had been strung with cages, their doors open, full of the exotic birds she allowed to fly about freely.

"Serena," I'd exclaimed. "But Serena's Serena and you told me she was a little bit highly strung."

"Yes, dear, I realise I told you that, but that was because you were too young to understand and now you're coming of age. We're not the only ones to be blessed like this, you know? Serena had it to a lesser extent and you know how dreadfully tragic that was since she was hopelessly, hopelessly drawn to the provocative and appealing world of evil darkness with dreadful consequences. This walking between worlds, this obsession with sex, well, we must remain balanced about it or it's bound to lead to madness."

This was a perplexing discussion for a birthday tea. Then again, I'd had a rather perplexing life living with Granny and being subjected to so much spiritual input.

Granny Rowena had gathered an eclectic mix of friends around her who she called her fellow travellers. In particular she'd been terribly fond of Serena Emerson, a woman of impeccable breeding, who at a young age, also held me in her thrall since she was an actress. Granny had loved Serena for her passion, uniqueness and her joie de vivre. She'd been terribly beautiful with dark bobbed hair and hugely appealing eyes running the whole gamut of emotions. However, Serena had fallen under the same spell of love and darkness that I would soon fall under.

Granny had met her at a theatre when Serena had been climbing the ladders of thespian success and starring in small stage productions. Granny had been enchanted by actors and Serena had been convincing probably because she lived her life like an illusion and therefore found an illusion easy to act. Serena, even then, had been possessed by a shadowy dark spectre, an entity who lived on the other side and who she said she was in love with. Poor Serena with her head half in and half out of dreams. I recall on one occasion at the height of her dark metamorphosis, she'd come to the house dressed in ivory, a stunning ermine stole around her neck, and instead of being her usual effusive self, Serena had been as white as a sheet and the flesh had melted from her bones, leaving her thin and ethereal. At that precise moment, she had not been doing so well with her acting career and over the last few months she'd lost a few parts because she'd become secretive and reclusive with no desire for earthly things, her ebullient personality masked by the greed and darkness cloaking her like a shadow. She had kept saying to Granny, "Oh, listen to me, listen to me, you don't know what it's like being taken in so many ways. It's a delicious thing. Your cunt doesn't know what it wants anymore and you feel like your soul has been turned inside out. I think in this way I can live forever, Rowena."

"Hush," Granny had said. "You don't want Emma to hear such crass vulgarity from a lady now, do you, Serena?"

Serena had pulled her ermine around her shoulders, and wobbling unsteadily on her feet and turning to me, she'd said, "I'd better warn you, dear. Love isn't what you read about in romantic novels. The real thing is nothing like that at all and I should know. Men's mortal fingers are cold and they're not artful. Men rush at sex without considering the virtues of a deeper connection. Affairs with a spirit are another thing entirely."

"I think that's enough, don't you?" Rowena had grumbled.

I hadn't cared. Granny had already explained to me that Serena was awfully unhappy in her marriage — and I knew such a lot about sex and even spirit sex that Serena's wanton remarks had just slithered off me like misfired arrows. Apparently, her husband had stifled her personality and made sex such an endurance that in the end Serena, pushed to the extreme and hankering for love and affection — had turned to her dark dreams and imaginings to find what she wanted. Gradually, Serena had lost interest in the human world completely, seeing it as little more than a shabby overcoat to be cast off. With the help of a dark spiritual guide she'd trained herself in devilish practices until she could bid her spirit leave her corporeal body at will in that act mystics like to call astral travel, thus journeying to the place inhabited by her lover, a jinni. She'd become obsessed with sex magic and conjurations of demon magic and thought that, through the marrying together of spirit and body, you could reach earth-shattering orgasms. In the end the pull of her spirit lover had proved irresistible and everybody thought poor Serena had been driven mad by her husband because she spent most of her time lying on her bed staring into the darkness obsessed by tortuous erotic dreams. One night she had been simply taken away to a home for the insane, a creepy old house that had doubled as a hospital in the war. Poor Serena.

"Do come along, aren't you going to eat that birthday cake?" Granny Rowena had winked at me as I'd dug my fork into my favourite lemon drizzle cake. "Then, since it's your eighteenth and quite a landmark, I must do two important things. The first is to show you your present and next I'll tell you something interesting." She had been staring at me intently. "My, you're going to be a beauty."

"Granny, I told you, I'm not pretty."

"But you are, dear, you're my little Pandora. God has to imbue everyone with something and you've been blessed with special charms. My dear, you have the sight but you also have an overpowering sexual allure that cannot be acquired. How lucky you are and what an incredible life you're going to have."

She'd bought me a trousseau of fabulous underclothes from Paris. There were silk knickers and corsets, and fine silk stockings and even a garter belt.

Granny's obsession with the naughty subject of sex controlled her. She'd spent a lot of her time preening and dressing herself to exquisite standards and she still entertained young men who were often found lounging around her home.

After this initial excitement, she had taken my hand and, kissing it and pressing it to her cheek, she'd sighed. "Darling, I can't believe you're eighteen and that's why it's important I talk to you. You see, I've had somewhat of a misspent youth. I've sinned on more than one occasion—almost as badly as poor Serena and the chances are you'll be tempted to sin in the same way. Yes, I've had spirit lovers and don't look at me like that." She adjusted the jet and amber beads around her neck. "Serena was always right in that respect—they make themselves known in a natural manner and it's the fate of our kind we can see into two worlds. They make the most fabulous lovers because, you see, unlike mortal man, they're endowed with spiritual presence. Everything's more considered, more satisfying, and, of course, every sensation is enhanced."

Granny had been apt to wander, but today her eyes had possessed the brightness and perspicacity of a teenager's.

I'd put my cup down with a rattle, staring at her in open-mouthed astonishment. "They say you can't make love to a ghost, though, they're too vaporous and their bodies are insubstantial so you pass straight through them," I'd observed.

"Poppycock." Rowena had laughed. "That's because the lover isn't on their level. With us it's different because we can walk between worlds and enter their world, somewhat like they can enter ours."

I can tell you I had first-hand knowledge of living in two worlds and it was both torture, pleasure and a prison of the senses. I seemed to be in a constant tug of war between on the one hand, the mortal world of my fleshy body with its fleshy delights, and the transcendental and magnetic pull of the other with its offerings of cosmic orgasmic bliss.

Chapter Three

"Emma, you're miles away."

"Yes." Still gazing in the mirror, I shook my head and snapping back to the present kissed Bem again, just to remind myself that I was alive and mortal but that in my arms I held a demon. His lips were sumptuous, full and velvety smooth, encouraging plunging tongues and a savouring of the warm vault.

"I understand these gestures are for yourself and if you want to torture yourself with the notion of human fingers in your cunt, you must do it," he grumbled. "So, I suppose I'll have to put up with imagining him with his hand on your hip whilst you dance."

"You're smudging my lipstick." Pushing Bem away gently, I picked up my fan and purse, and not a moment too soon, because right then I heard the toot of David's car horn. I'd told him to wait in the car and on no account was he to come and call for me. If he found this request strange he hadn't said so, but there again he loved me, and love forgave everything.

I came down the steps of Langhousa holding up the hem of my shimmering gown so I didn't accidentally trip and David opened the car door for me. In his dinner suit with a long silk scarf, he was beautiful — or as beautiful as a human could be, and I felt a faint tug, but only a tug of what could be termed lust.

"Dear Emma." He kissed my hand. "So, you've given yourself a night off on good behaviour after all. You know, I expected a call right up until the last minute to say you'd changed your mind."

"David, I'm many things. But, even you have to admit I never let anyone down." The instant I was in the car I felt bad about what I was doing and the touch of David's hand reminded me of the feel of an icicle I'd once snapped off the shed roof when I was a child back in England. It burnt with the touch of my lover but it was a different kind of burning — the unpleasant feeling of human flesh and not a demon's. I moved my hands away, clasping my pretty beaded purse.

"Always so fragile." He studied me out of the corner of his eye, a perplexed expression on his face. "You're so fascinating and that's why I think I love you so much. You're so sexual and yet so naïve, so frigid at times and yet so hot." His glance slithered over me. "Look at you, gorgeous girl, what a gown. It suits you to perfection. However, darling, despite looking divine, you've lost a little weight." His gaze drifted to the strands of pearls. "Wearing Wilberta's pearls too, I see? Goodness, they show off your neck so well I can't stop staring at you." He laughed. "I'll have an accident if I don't concentrate."

He pulled the car over onto the grass just before the front gate, and kissing my fingers, turned my hand over with his own. The skin was now so transparent you could see the patterning of blue veins. I realised then I was transforming before everyone's eyes.

"Come along, a little peck right here, for old time's sake." He touched the hollow right under the dimple on his cheek. "I don't believe you're an ice maiden, you're made of sex and you know it, although to my knowledge you've never dated anyone more than once or twice. Why is that, I wonder? I was trying to work it out earlier today. Are you actually afraid of sex?" He was appraising me? "I find that slightly hard to believe."

I glanced out of the window before turning to kiss him. "There, will that satisfy you?" I knew that Bem was probably hiding in the bushes watching me. He could dart from place to place with the speed of light, until he felt the cord of imprisonment that jerked him back. I had yet to fully understand the conditions of his mysterious incarceration within the box and how its curse had erected an invisible etheric prison wall. It was of such power and complexity that he could never break its spell and was destined to wander only a short distance from its confines.

The other funny thing was, the moment we turned out of the gates of Langhousa, it was as if the tether threading all the way back to Bem had snapped tight with so pronounced a sensation I gasped and, gripping my seat, bent double with pain. When I looked in the rear mirror and saw my face drained of colour, it reminded me it was true and that I no longer existed fully within the mortal world because my heart and soul belonged to a demon.

Chapter Four

It was a lovely restaurant—the tables shaded by small lamps and a quintet playing delightful soft music in the corner. I turned my face towards the musicians, letting the atmosphere wash all over me. Before the other world claimed me I had never been so supersensitive. Now, I felt like I could become a musical note or a vibrating atom of air.

I ate little because everything was so distracting, bright and loud. And anyway, food seemed to turn to ashes in my mouth, it was so bland compared to the demon food I now dined out on. All eyes were on me, watching every forkful I consumed, and no wonder, since I was one of the most eligible English women in Chandrapoor and rather a spectacle, being a recluse. That evening, tugging gently against Bem's silken mental handcuffs, I knew I'd lost the battle. I was no longer simple Emma Spence, but a sinful, despicable creature, craving a demon's world. *I'm wicked, wicked,* I thought, *and I may as well surrender.*

"You see how truly fabulous you are, Emma? You're an angel, everyone's admiring you, men and women alike."

David was trying so hard to flatter me and make me happy, because he still hoped I might love him, I could tell that he did. He understood how timid I was in social situations and he was being excessively kind to choose a table in the corner away from everyone, where we could be an island on our own. I felt warmth and the prickle of distant desire—a faint prickle and that was all. A human man could never warm my senses in the way a demon could and yet still he tried, although I was as cold as ice. Despite the constant chatter and the crash of knives and forks and the feeling of a world caving in on me and crushing me, there was still some pleasure in observing human activity. I gazed around with girlish enthusiasm, even managing to eat a small slice of birthday cake to please him.

David treated me similar to a fragile invalid since he thought me so chaste and a little damaged, and he wasn't alone. Society was under the misapprehension I was a virgin, and I had been until that day with Shankar in the Formentosa hotel where he took my virginity with exquisite finesse. Lord knows, until that moment, I'd had enough close encounters with men who'd wanted to touch me and get their hands on my flesh and, I'd enjoyed it well enough until they'd attempted to undress me. Presented with the tool that they so flagrantly displayed, and after a bit of poking and prodding, the fires within me were dulled to the barest remnant of embers. Then I'd become tight and resisting, a cold alabaster statue. The men in turn had become angry and had called me many dreadful things like 'tease' and 'whore' and 'frigid lunatic'. It had been different with Shankar because he had carried me on his spiritual tide and had instructed me in the ways of libidinous seduction I'd fantasised about. And now with Bem it was infinitely different.

I stared across the table, clenching my fists. There was no getting away from it, I was finding this world stranger by the day and I disdained human. These mortal men did not see the world that Shankar and Bem inhabited, and as a result, it made them seem one dimensional and grey. David was the exception to the rule because he was a little bit different. He'd never been a gutsy, sexy man and there was the barest garnish of the spiritual about him that excited me. On occasion, he could be dreamy, sensual and very romantic and I suppose, in other circumstances, I'd have found a good companion in him. The trouble was I'd walked for far too long on the other side and I'd felt the taste on my tongue of something tantalising. Shankar had been reborn only a while in Bem, but already I'd tasted enough demon sin and learnt enough about demon love to realise it was now the only love to draw the lust out from the dark shadows of my consciousness. And, I knew a fair amount about lust. Despite my supposed frigidity and my hatred of mortal fingers and cock, I craved sex and I knew the extent of enjoyment my own fingers and a dildo purchased in an Indian bazaar could give me. Even when I was a young woman I'd made love to the dark spirit of my imagination and it had excited me more than any mortal flesh could.

David observed me carefully whilst he recited all the society news. He told me about the trouble with the tribesmen up north and about Mrs Fassbender's arthritis, before somehow the subject came around again to marriage and he was smiling and saying,

"You realise you can't be alone in that big old house, Emma, it isn't the thing to do, is it? Women don't live alone, not nice, decent women, beautiful women." He squeezed my hand persuasively. "Come along, darling. Although you won't admit it, you know you need me and we would get along very well. I'm somewhat timid myself regarding sex and I'd let you take it at your own pace, we needn't even sleep together at first. You see how dreadfully amenable I am?"

"Oh, for goodness' sake, David. What a terrible suggestion," I retorted, trying to disentangle myself.

"Terrible? I don't see why. You're evidently a vital woman, a woman of fire, and I'm willing to be patient and give you what you want. You realise the sensible thing to do is get married, even if it's simply to allay the gossip. The whole of Chandrapoor society looks at you from behind a frosted glass of suspicion, my dear. They call you an occultist, a crazy woman... Well, I could banish that with my good name. Marry a good financier and I'll make you respectable."

I stared at his hand lying in mine, a square mortal hand, and I tried to find some electrical arousal in the strength of the capability of it, but I couldn't. Nothing as simple as feeble human desire could excite me like it once had. Bem's tether would always be the strongest, the hardest to snap and my world had changed and moved around me in slow waves. Mortal things touched me with a distant echo—a prodding of dense earthly fingers as the world fought to reclaim me and loosen the silken demon restraints on my wrists and around my ankles. Gritting my teeth in trembling orgasm, I felt it now, the tether squeezing to remind me, remind me of who I was.

David stared at me queerly. "Are you all right? You seem feverish."

"Yes."

He turned my wrist, his brow furrowed and I watched his finger dancing down the long red line. "Good Lord, what's this, what's this terrible mark?"

I peered at my wrist. To be honest I'd entirely forgotten the marks made by the invisible webs of bondage, but there they were, one world seeking to impinge upon the other — Bem's world enforcing and leaving a distinct print of evidence. I enjoyed them and I liked to rub them from time to time to cause that warm arousing burn. Yes, I took a distinct pleasure from it. I giggled childishly. "Oh these, they're nothing. I was helping Anya do some tying in the garden and some twine got caught around my wrist."

David considered this. He was such a good man he was bound to take my word for it. In his view, what else could they be, anyway? It would never cross his mind what these marks represented, namely my esoteric bondage, the chains of lust held by my salacious dark master. He sat back in his chair, shrugging his slim shoulders. "Well then, there we are, you see. That simply underlines my theory. This is precisely why a woman like you should be married. You live in a rambling great house with aged servants who date back to your great-grandmother's day. You need someone to take care of you."

"Why should a woman get married for those reasons?" Anger spiralled, making me feel giddy.

"Most women get married. I know it's the nineteen-twenties and the female of the species thinks she's won herself a great deal of liberty, but women are designed to be married and cared for."

I glared at him. "How old-fashioned of you. Are we too fragile, is that what you think? Can't we manage our own finances, be independent? Do you think in my case Langhousa will drop down around my ears?"

"Darling, darling, I didn't mean to provoke such a reaction. Please." He was leaning forward earnestly. "Forgive me, sweetheart. How clumsy of me. Honest to God, I didn't mean to offend you, especially on your birthday. You know how I can be clumsy with words." He kissed my hand. "I'm making a really bad job of explaining. All I want to do is provide a safe harbour for you and to love you and look after you. I was born to care for you, don't you realise that? When I first saw you with your grandmother when you were sixteen, I looked at you and I thought, she's so stunning, the angel. I have to have her and I could make her so happy. I've made you happy tonight, haven't I?"

I knew what I next had to say would be exceedingly hard, but I couldn't mislead him, I couldn't.

"Yes, yes you've made me happy, David. The thing is I don't think I can make you happy, I really don't and I don't want you to"—I looked down at my plate—"have any hope, because I won't change my mind."

Chapter Five

When I came back to Langhousa, I dropped my purse on the table and, leaning my hip against the heavy piece of furniture, I thought about bursting into tears. It was an ill-considered thing I'd done. I'd badly upset the one person in my life who at least understood me a little. David was wounded and he'd hardly spoken to me on the journey back.

Two lamps were burning low, casting a faint light over the walls. They were the only lights on in the house and the moths attracted to them flittered in through the open window, bumping against the glass. I turned my head, my senses so acutely attuned to the ethers that I could hear the flutter of their tiny paper-thin wings.

Bem was watching me from the shadows again, as much a part of the shadows as they were themselves. His eyes glistened with the usual thirst—his thirst for flames and fire and my bare skin that raised his lust like mercury in a barometer. I shivered with a mixture of fear and longing. So what if he saw fit to punish me, I deserved it and although I hated to admit it I wanted that punishment. I glanced down at the table and saw that a glass of champagne with jasmine petals floating on top had been placed right where he knew I would see it. There was enough of Shankar in him to remember it would remind me of the Formentosa hotel all those months ago when he was as mortal as I was, and not this dark, heathen angel. I picked up the glass, turning the stem in my fingers, raising it to my lips and swallowing the sweet liquid in one greedy gulp.

"Darling." He emerged from the shadows, his face all hard angles with a twist of bitterness to his lips. Bem was a curtain of flickering fire, his evil dark charm making me breathless. "It's so late, I wondered if you would come back or, if somehow he'd managed to get his hands on your cunt and had taken you home to seduce you. Did you have a wonderful dinner?"

I'd forgotten to lock the sinful treasure box before I'd left the house. But, it was getting harder and harder to remember things with my resolve melting under the persuasive caress of his sex and the heady otherworldly atmosphere of a house impregnated by lust. Every time I touched the keys hanging around my neck, Bem would get on his hands and knees, and naked, kiss my feet and beg me not to do it, not to shut him back in his dark, enchanted prison. It was hard to punish someone you loved, especially when you had a yearning to possess them and they were a part of you and you wanted them, felt them flowing through your veins every second of every day.

"Bem, don't be disgusting. David and I argued a little and it made me late, that's all."

He caught hold of me, twisting my hair around his wrist, and I eased myself into the delicious pain with a barely audible sigh of delight, resting my head on his shoulder while the most careful of lovers - he cradled me tenderly, his palm circling the small of my back. A frisson of excitement, warm and dancing and endlessly enticing made my heart skip a beat. Not to be outdone by David, he'd donned his finery and now wore the suit I'd first seen Shankar in at the Formentosa hotel — one of the best from a fine Calcutta tailors and that hugged his contours. He was determined to parade his butterfly colours and make David seem a drab moth in comparison. Bem found clothes such an odd attribute of human vanity and he continually tugged and pulled at them, fighting the fabric that clung to him like a badly fitting skin. He much preferred his naked demon skin, and to be truthful so did I because his was a body to salivate over, one created to seduce mortal woman.

His full lips nuzzled my ear. "Did it feel good to betray me, Emma? Was it like being a naughty schoolgirl climbing from the dormitory window and sneaking out to see your lover, or shall I put it another way? Was it similar to a piercing hot needle between your legs?"

"No, it wasn't like that. Christ, you can be so, so...dirty. Actually, after tonight, I think David must hate me and he has good reason to when he could tell I was having orgasms every five minutes and evidently it wasn't due to him." I tugged myself free of his embrace, then crossed my arms and wandered to the French doors. I pushed them wide and stepped out onto the veranda, sitting down defiantly on one of the rattan chairs.

After a while I could feel Bem's stare on the back of my neck, and when I glanced up he was watching me.

"You're wasted on that ridiculous social set, Emma. You're worth a thousand of the Mrs Fassbenders and

Rowena Montagues and no mortal man could appreciate you the way I do." Coming up behind me, he tipped my head back, removing my loose hair combs, stroking my skin and fanning my hair out in a spider's web nimbus around my shoulders. "Surrender to my world, darling, it'll be so much easier in the long run, than this constant denial, this constant inner war."

Turning my face into his palm, I kissed it, absorbing the demon smells of copal, resin and dark enchantment, feeling myself melt, become liquid. Surrendering seemed preferable to this constant battle, my mind snapping one more mortal tether as it struggled to float free.

"Let me unbutton that gown." He was gazing hungrily at the sheer silk of my dress. "You know how I love to undress you."

Bem got to his knees in front of me, slipping open the row of pearl buttons. Easing back the fabric, he kissed my shoulders, and sucking my skin, grazed it with his teeth so I exploded in orgasmic shivers. Well, I conjectured, it had been fun to try and see if satisfaction existed outside the prison of Langhousa, but my prison was much more than four walls, it was the prison of my mind and body. How could I have imagined that a dose of enforced mortal medicine could have somehow quenched the indecent, sublime delights existing here in Bem's arms and which made David's love a feeble companion to such thrilling darkness?

As the warm unfolding veil of energies draped themselves over me and I became quivering and feverish, I realised only Bem could give me what I needed. From this moment there would be no outside world—there was only one world and it was the world I'd fashioned for myself.

"You won't go again, will you?" he begged, kissing me and sliding his warm tongue against mine. "Promise me, Emma?"

The gown fell forwards, revealing more of my shoulders. "No, I don't think I will, and anyway you've woven so many silken strands around me I'm imprisoned by your queer power." I stared at my wrists and ankles and wondered how these invisible tethers only the demon spider weaver was able to spin, could hold me in such subtle erotic bondage, but they did. Often he secured me to a chair or bed post with them and fed on me, stretching the skeins around my tossing, naked body and playing with me as he teased my flesh into rigid, quivering, orgasmic bliss. I felt molten just at the thought of those woven strands pulling on my body and cunt, the silky tendrils wringing the sex from my corporeal form.

I'm certain people knew that I was somehow destroyed and undergoing this erotic corruption, because the guilty secret was written all over my face and I smelt strongly of sex—the heady demon sex clinging to my thighs—the sticky issue giving me such a perverse thrill that I seldom washed it off.

"I sent my net. Did you feel me, Emma?" Bem began his seductive magical incantation—calling on the elements of earth, air, fire and water to possess me.

"I felt you all over me." I quavered, the familiar creeping warmth nestling at the base of my spine.

Sliding his hands under my knees, he lifted me, limp as a ragdoll, and carried me back inside the house and into the bedroom where he pulled out a chair and sat me down in front of my cheval mirror. I'd been holding my gown across my chest and I let it go to expose my pendant breasts with their violet-hennaed nipples. I'd fallen easily into these despicable pagan ways and there was something dirty about this whorish reddening. What delight he'd taken in touching a brush to my fevered skin and licking the tips into fire. I liked the painting immensely, the flaring nubs vivid against my white alabaster flesh. He'd been down between my legs too, stroking his herbal brew onto dewy sex lips vivid as purple bougainvillea.

He was watching me in the mirror, his eyes glistening with demonic intent. Such a face had been designed by an evil god to melt my insides. On Shankar's warm and mortal body those features had been striking and godlike enough. Sharpened now by the demon, they were irresistible signposts of lust and seduction, simmering with salacious promise. I was powerless to resist my immortal charmer and what's more I knew I was feeding him—feeding him every day with my mortal woman's sex and desire. This thought gave me a sensation of both satisfaction and terror—terror that I allowed myself to be captive in such a situation of bondage, satisfaction that my mortal love was his catharsis, the driving force for his sexual metamorphosis. One thing was for sure, I could no more give up this lusty poison now than an addict could give up an opium pipe.

"Emma." His whisper was like the breeze through the rustling leaves and it made the hairs on my body stand erect and my nipples form into tight kernels. "It was torture imagining you in his arms."

He dragged me to my feet and, placing his hand in the small of my back, he ground his sinuous body against mine, making sure I felt every inch of him. "I couldn't bear it, sitting in the darkness, aching for you.

To preserve my sanity I imagined you sitting naked and entertaining me at the piano in the way you generally do, all that gorgeous flesh on show and that place between your legs open, wet and ready for me to feed on whilst you seduced me with a sweet sonata. I was in a frenzy wondering if those ties to the mortal world you talk about would somehow be strong, strong enough to draw you back." He nuzzled my throat. "Truly, I was eaten up with jealousy."

He continued easing the gown down my body until it slithered in a pile around my feet, the tiny hand-stitched crystal beads glistening in the moonlight. I was hot and fluid, my legs gaping. I moved them apart and he unclipped my suspenders, caressing each of my legs and pulling down my wet stockings whilst my juices trickled. I reached up to loosen the pearl necklace.

"Oh no, leave it on."

I turned the glistening pearls in my fingers. They were exceedingly lovely and I'd always admired them. Every time my mother had put them on I'd stared at them and wondered how something natural could be so beautiful. I'd once hankered for lots of earthly mortal things—satin and fur and diamonds and even the taste of champagne and men's admiring glances—but I coveted very little anymore and only wore the pearls because I knew it gave Bem a great deal of joy to see the dark stains shimmering against my paleness. Now, I'd gladly swap them for gossamer webs of bondage or the glitter of demon cum on fevered skin.

Savage darts of pleasure stabbed me here and there.

"You're a wicked woman, Miss Emma Spence. You're so wicked, wicked in such an innocent way it drives me crazy."

I remembered the long afternoons when I had laid in bed at the Formentosa hotel with Shankar and had talked about, heaven forbid, what would happen if one or the other of us should perish. Even then I had a strong intuitive feeling fate had a cruel twist in store for us but I also had a feeling we were meant to be together for eternity.

Bem's fingers were dancing over my skin, lighting me here and there before he followed them with his mouth, biting gently to the point of pain. I sizzled with anticipation, knowing this foreplay would soon have me begging him for all manner of heinous persecutions of the flesh. He'd made me into a twisted bitch and I wanted sex of a more cunning and deeper nature than the weak mortal thing most women craved. I wanted the warm unfolding serpent to creep up my spine, darting out tendrils of venom, exploding in my head in ripples of such profound ecstasy I would scream and beat my fists on the bedcovers. Yes, I stared into the black mirrors of his eyes. I wanted it. My mind was full now of slippery wet writhing images. How stupidly out of place clothing seemed on a spirit body, as he struggled with human design, each button and fastening alien to him. Peeling off his shirt, he let it fall from his muscular bronzed shoulders and what I now thought of, as his long demon fingers next unbuttoned his pants, releasing that demon part of him that made me melt to see it, since I knew what joy it could give me. I was pleasantly devoid of strength, Bem easing his fingers in my mouth so I could bite and nibble. The wet swollen length of him quivered and hardened against my leg. I put my hand on his and moved it everywhere, letting it linger and tantalise whilst he coated me in a blanket of fire and his demon fingers reclaimed me from the world of mortal.

"Oh," I moaned, unashamedly, the invisible silken threads tightening at wrist and ankle. "Tighter, Bem."

Teasing me all over with his tongue, he began fondling the erogenous zones behind my ears—his hands inching up the insides of my thighs. Continuing to prod around my plump fleshy mound, he was a demon thief stealing my emotions. Gradually, he drew me down deeper into a well of turbulent drowning desire, probing between my pouting vermillion lips to reveal my clit—a delectable morsel for his demon appetite. My entire body was shaking in convulsions of joy as I exploded in perfect syncopation with the deluge from above and the heavens opened, the full force of a sudden monsoon downpour hammering against the roof, knocking open the doors with supernatural force. Afterwards, raindrops scattered the floor in scintillating diamond strings and I watched them trembling and vibrating, animated with the life of jinn spirits, soaking the delicate embroidered chairs and glimmering like clitoral gems. I ran my fingers through his soft hair. How easy it was to forget he was not a man.

"Emma, my darling," he murmured, concentrating on my pleasure. "Don't you see, you don't need that world anymore?"

"But, I am that world, Bem, I'll always be mortal."

"Maybe so." He was frowning again. "But, darling, even so, you could belong in my world too." He licked my ear, cradling me and stroking my body, his voice becoming coaxing and more bewitching. "Did you think about throwing away the keys and releasing me so I'm no longer a prisoner? It's worse than any filthy Calcutta jail in there."

"Well, we're even then," I said. "Because you hold me in a prison of the senses." I put my hands to my cheeks, feeling the flicker of his energies over my skin as my fine hair, propelled by his electromagnetism, tickled my face. I was finding it increasingly hard to concentrate under the protracted attention of his caresses.

"Wouldn't you like me to be here forever to read you the Rubaiyat of Omar Kayam, and to wake in the morning next to you, to talk and amuse you, Emma? We're the truest of lovers, married in heart and soul. How can you keep your husband captive?" He bit my lip fiercely and the lust surged. "My darling, you know you yearn for that dirty blissful place of ecstatic hell only a demon can give you. Well, I have yet to bind you in fire and light you with exquisite craving. Give me what I want and I'll give you the surprises I have in store for you."

"You monster, you blackmail me." I shuddered with anger. "We've had this ridiculous conversation before, but you'll have to make the best of it, I can't live in two worlds. It's impossible and someone would notice. You realise everyone watches and conspires and at the first sign of madness they'd have me consigned to that awful madhouse. I can't allow the spirit world to consume me." What a truly depraved pair we were, I thought studying his implacable expression. "Aren't you happy to have your mistress like this, divine Bem? You have me to yourself most of the time after all."

He kissed my lips, his gaze moving to the keys on the long thin chain around my neck. He daren't touch them because they were so imbued with magic they'd burn his demon skin. I kept them artfully concealed, tucking them down beneath my décolletage, hidden from prying eyes.

"Emma, I want to love you completely, whenever and wherever I choose. I despise the way you cling to human. Why not give me those keys, lover? Allow me to properly be your master in the place of those scandalmongers and gossips. I adore you and it would be so easy for us since you're as reclusive as your grandmother. You don't entertain, you don't socialise, you despise those chatterboxes, so why are you intent on preserving your humanness and telling me it's a sacrifice to deny this world of illusion? We all have to sacrifice something. Take Vasi for instance. The man was like a brother and a father to me when I was mortal. Do you think it's easy for me when I see him sitting on the step looking so crestfallen about my mortal death? No, dear, it isn't. I wish I could run to him and embrace him and say, 'Here's Shankar, your spiritual son.' But I know I cannot for both our sakes."

"It's ridiculous, utterly ridiculous to keep having this argument." I was losing my temper, my voice rising higher. "Only I can see you, and how would it seem if I strolled through the house muttering to myself and talking to shadows. Oh, Bem, for goodness' sake." I jumped up angrily to latch the door, which was rocking now from another heavy assault of rain. "You're no longer a mortal man. Anya can't see you. No one can see you except me and others like me. Why do you torment me with this? We're both of us trapped in a manner of speaking. Me, in my warm human body and you in your fiery spirit world and because of that we're forced to make the best of it." I clapped my hands to my head. "And please, Bem, stop looking for the book. I know you've been to all my hiding places moving my clothes, searching, always searching, and you won't find it."

Bem knew I never took the two precious keys to the sinful box of treasure from around my neck. However, he was intent on finding the third key, hidden in the Holy Book of Ravrankar and which I'd made sure I'd hidden in a very safe place indeed, and where I knew he wouldn't find it.

"My darling Emma." He came strolling after me as sinuous as a panther, his incredibly alluring body filling me once more with lust. Backing me up against the wall, he combed his hands through my hair, before savagely jerking my head back. Oh pain, more pain, how could I stand it? I'd been so fearful of it once. Now, by my own admission I wanted to beg him for more. His finger slid inside my warm tunnel—he knew I couldn't resist his seduction. I shaved my skin to polished perfection for him and his fingers lingered over my smooth scented skin, touching, feeling. "Yes of course you're right, darling, and I realise it's bad of me to keep searching around for that book, but despite the joys of submitting to a gorgeous gaoler you don't know what it's like being a prisoner for so many centuries in such a dark prison." He winked at me slyly. "That Pandora's box of sins is a house of reprobates who chatter endlessly and whose voices drive me to distraction. You loved me in mortal life, now you withhold my freedom from me. Turn to the darkness, Emma, love me devotedly, unconditionally, like I do you."

"It's simply that you cannot abide being at my beck and call, can you?" I ground out as, easing me open, he groped around my vulva. Oh, damn this weakness for sex. I turned my head away, pressing it to the wall. I was sinking deeper and deeper into depraved longing, defenceless against the burning trail of his touch. "How much trickery will you use to force me to free you? And anyway, even if I did give you the keys you could never wander far from Ravrankar's box. The magic surrounding it is far too strong. You told me yourself that Ravrankar's magic holds you and if you stray farther than the grove of *bodhi* trees the white angels will mercilessly round you up and thrash you with their whips of fire."

Bem smirked at me. "Ah, sweetheart, those cords of magic. I'm already working on ways to snap them."

He was an elemental orgasmic hunter stalking his prey and I had no strength left to resist. Instead I waited, loose and vibrating, for the touch of his lips, tongue and finger whilst he pressed against me, sniffing and licking me all over like an animal. It was intensely erotic as his demon antenna detected my simmering orgasm and patiently nurtured it.

I slithered to the floor and we tossed and turned, consuming one another, exploring one another's dips and hollows. His skin was so alluring, gleaming and virgin smooth, his balls tightening to lift his brazen, upwardly thrusting cock—a triumph of the gods. I was rapidly forgetting the ride to the restaurant with David's hand on my neck teasing a curl of hair. Forgetting the hushed silence as I'd walked inside on his arm and saw the sparkling cutlery and crystal glass and David glancing at me with no jealousy in his eyes, only admiration.

Bem blew his breath all over me, coaxing the embers of my desire until pleasure burst over me in licking fingers of flame. I was powerless, a simple observer of my tortured passion, as enraptured and removed from myself, I floated miles above my body.

"Give it to me." I moaned, deliciously entangled with him, spasms rippling through my womb. It was like I was becoming a germinating seed, which at any moment was going to burst open in a fecund act of sexual transformation. "Give it to me."

I ran my finger down his corded muscle, his long strands of black hair tickling my breasts, his lips curving into a merciless grin. The fact he wielded so much power over me only made me more aroused.

"Do you see them, Emma?" Raising his hands, he proceeded to show me the curious etheric chains he wove before binding me hand, foot and sex. Glimmering in the light, they were ephemeral, almost invisible. I sighed. I wanted his hands back touching me and I didn't want to waste a minute. I'd learnt the hands of a demon were not like any man's, they had the power to arouse you in subtle ways and they were smooth, oh yes, so smooth. There weren't any lines of life or death to mark the palm, although mysteriously they were warm. What a puzzle this spirit was.

I realised what I'd done. Every day I battled with myself, attempting to push the niggling doubts to the back of my head. After all, wasn't I responsible for his creation, hadn't my lusty greed driven me to seek him within the fabric of dark enchantment? For just a second I experienced a pang of fear — it returned from time to time, jabbing at me with its needle-sharp reminder that Bem was and could never be a man. He was an interloper, a vampire of love, devouring mortal desires like a gourmand dines out on his favourite food. There was no escaping the fact I'd been selfish and done a dark thing. Every time I kissed him I had to convince myself that in my bed I had a visitor, a body of dark design, the creation of the conjuror Mr Bodekar.

I shuddered. Spinning the webs between the loom of his fingertips, he swaddled me in bliss, my skin sending skittering signals all over my body. Laughing, he was leaning over me, brushing my lips with his, whispering in my ear, "You naughty girl leaving me like that, Emma. I will show you who's your lord and master."

"Show me," I implored, running my tongue over my lips. "Make me scream."

Perhaps, I ought to transgress more often, so that I can suffer this exquisite punishment.

Ensnared in a world of sex, taken to new erotic heights and a submissive within his licentious thrall, I was losing sight of my world. Devilish spider, he had now cocooned me, and my wrists and ankles were connected to the heavy wooden legs of the bureau at my feet and the upholstered couch against the wall at my head. Splayed and tied for his delectation, the reclaiming of my body back from that of mortal began with him licking me clean of the world of David, with fiery sweeps of his tongue.

* * * *

Much later, I woke up in my bed then, swinging my legs over the side, I got up. I stepped out onto the veranda and leaning over the edge turned my face up to the clouds and opened my mouth so the jinn spirit of the rain could flow down my cheeks and skin. I gulped it down thirstily, allowing the elemental rain spirit to drive me to the precipice of thrilling ecstasy with drifting jinn raindrops. It was always like this following sex with Bem and it was becoming worse. His love sensitised me and drew me into a world of a million heightened sensations, into a primitive elemental wonder where everything possessed needle-sharp clarity and feelings were magnified a thousand times. The rain plastered my hair to my head and spiralled in rivulets down my naked body and I shuddered from the orgasmic detonations, knees quaking, my body vibrating. A lizard fixed me with its beady eye. Running across my foot it made me flare, clenching my toes. I rubbed my hands over my body, sighing whilst I enjoyed the lingering soreness from so much sex, realising even now that I wanted his demon lips on me yet again. For the moment how tempting a dip in the sacred pool at the bottom of the garden would be, soothing me, damping down the heat racing through my veins.

I ran helter-skelter down the path towards the pool, moving whilst in a mental haze. Reaching the bushes I pushed my way through the dripping foliage, aware of the sounds of the jungle, the whisper of unfurling fronds and sprouting mosses and the cloying rich scents beneath the fabric of the mortal world. Even the earth felt alive and I sunk my toes into it. I frequently came down to this pool, immersing myself in the waters from the stream cascading down from the holy hills, hoping that somehow their spiritual purity could extinguish the burning lust inside my womb, swirl away the evil juices of my demon lord. Because, despite my love for him I knew I was a sinner and every day I waged a mental battle whilst he slowly erased my humanness a little bit more.

Reaching the bank, I dropped down onto my knees and, rubbing my hands over my body, I lay writhing, gripped by fingers of energy, the naughty jinn spirits crowding towards me in flickering beads of light. They danced from leaf to leaf hovering above me like tiny bursts of spirit energy. I shook myself and combed my fingers through my hair, before I stood up, and advancing cautiously, sunk down into the water, spreading my limbs out for its cool embrace, while the liquid folded around me in a living cloak. After such torrid lust with Bem this vital water felt so good, everything did. Every day I was aware of my heightened sensitivities. They stimulated my awakening self and were enough to send me into a climactic fever. For example, the touch of my brush when combing my hair, the pulling on of my clothes, but most of all the natural elemental things — the soft caress of the breeze, the cooling swirl of water. Natural things were jinn, they were of the elemental world and because of this they retained echoes and complex energy patterns.

I couldn't help it and I submerged myself, whimpering at the feel of those fingers creeping inside me. I opened my legs and, kicking out from the bottom of the pool I let myself float, legs akimbo, the open opalescent petals of a lily, the refracted light highlighting the tips of my nails which had now taken on the hue of nacreous oyster shell, my long hair spreading out around me in a pale rippling fan.

I was reluctant to leave this alluring orgasmic ocean of perpetual arousal and I could have drifted forever, my body gently convulsing, weeds tickling my ankles with silken fingers, the water nibbling my sex like an impatient lover. Eventually though, I swam towards the edge, striking out with lazy strokes and slicing through the water before climbing out. I sat on the bank wringing out my long skeins of hair and twisting them into a knot.

* * * *

When I returned to the bungalow I stood for a moment, my attention caught by the sinful treasure box on the table. Despite my fear of it I didn't know why I felt drawn to it so much, but I always had. I let my fingers trail over the carvings. It was both terrifying and so ancient. Ever since Shankar first showed me the box I'd been baffled by it. The box entranced me with its esoteric emptiness. It was truly a thing of magic, wrought by the gods. Lifting the lid, I cautiously peered inside seeing that the interior was lit by the usual unearthly glow and from out of it escaped smoky wisps of etheric substance. I splayed my fingers, confounded, wondering why I could never seem to feel the bottom or sides, which were as dark and fathomless as Hades. The errant jinn spirits attracted by the elemental power of my jinn lord rose from the saturnine depths to cluster around my hands, leaping and twisting in dancing pinpoints of orange flame with hearts of sapphire. Swarming over my fingers and nibbling like little fishes, they left their soft kisses.

Yes, this sinful treasure box was the bottle for my magical genie or – as Bem kept reminding me – his infernal prison. Dropping the lid, I stood back, fingering the keys around my neck, rubbing my thumb over the intricate design. Who was I becoming? Because I seemed to revel in the growing power I had over Bem. With these keys, I controlled the doorway to ecstasy and I could cross into Bem's fiery world of delight whenever I chose to by releasing him, although more and more often I sought not to summon him back to the box. However, I also realised that, although I held the keys of dominion over him, more and more I knew he worked deviously to control me. Day by day, my mind was becoming mesmerised by this dark denizen and now I was tethered to this mortal world by only the thinnest of threads. Bem wandered through the dark rooms of Langhousa — my family's large old plantation bungalow — incongruous in his human finery, touching my clothes and stroking me.

"Emma, there you are, sweetheart," he whispered, and I shivered as he came up behind me, his expert hands once again on my wet flesh, stroking me, coming between my legs — his hand already squeezing my sex. He turned me around, backing me up against the table. He was like a priapic god with his smooth muscular skin and his penis jutting aggressively forward, grazing my leg.

I stretched my arms and legs, luxuriating in my body's responses. "Mmm, Bem."

"Emma, you're soaking and still human enough to die of pneumonia, whatever have you been doing?"

"I felt possessed and I went down to the pool in the rain. You see what you're doing? You're driving me crazy with your world."

After snatching my robe from the back of a chair, he next rubbed me dry while I stood meekly, enjoying the feel of his hands. "Come, let's sit outside on the veranda, it's so humid." Gathering some cushions off the couch, he threw them down on the veranda and we laid touching and fondling one another. Eventually, the silver goddess moon emerged from behind the ragged tatters of cloud, bathing everything in silvery light and painting the garden in lunar-tinted magic. I loved being outside like this listening to the rustling in the branches and with the canopy of stars and constellations above our heads. Fireflies moved amongst the flowers like shimmering beacons of hope and I saw Bem's dark gaze shifted around the undergrowth with interest. He pressed his finger to his lips, smiling because more jinn spirits were creeping out of their hiding places. They'd come to see the lord of the jinn clothed in his new human finery.

"Emma, you'll love me for eternity, won't you?" Bending across, he licked my ear, gently before biting the lobe.

I giggled. "Oh, Bem, don't do that. Of course I will. What makes you say such a thing?"

The long locks of black hair fell forwards over his eyes, giving him the look of a naughty street urchin. "Ah, because you're still a mortal, Emma, and a stunning woman and all men want you, even more so since you became touched by fire."

Drawing my knees up, I stroked his skin. His human shell — truly a thing of magic, wrought by the gods and possessed by this raunchy devil spirit felt burning to the touch and when I kissed him his tongue in my mouth was liquid fire.

Last week when he'd been sleeping I'd cut a lock of his raven black hair for my locket but strangely the hair had died and turned grey within minutes. This was a definite sign of magic at work. Not that I'd needed proof of what he was anyway — he was not Shankar but he was a part of Shankar.

When Shankar had died I'd stolen his soul and in my grief I'd gone to see Mr Bodekar, an artist at weaving the ethers. Mr Bodekar had conjured a human body, so vital and glowing and so identical to Shankar I had been fooled. The hair, the skin, the body of my lover, all of it was an artful illusion, a magical cocoon for the legendary Bem Hazari.

"Command me and I'll go." Bem pouted, offering his delectable lips for another kiss. "Pick up the despised keys and make it so, for you itch to send me back to that blasted box."

"You're imagining things. Can demons be this paranoid?" Pulling a face, I looked up at him, then I burst out laughing. His soulful eyes, black as night and large reflective mirrors, gazed into mine.

He stroked the crease between my eyebrows. "Don't frown, darling, I know everything. I know all about the conniving you and your psychic friend Merkel have spoken in secret." He touched my third eye, that mysterious blind spot to humans, and my mind exploded in shards of light. "Tomorrow you plan on setting out for Pamlakar, to the sacred place known by my forefathers. Do you recall the cricket who's always sitting on the table and singing to you? Well, all the creatures of earth, air, fire and water obey me and he told me long ago you intended to betray me."

Betrayed by a cricket — it made me want burst out giggling — but my heart plummeted. I'd been so sure I'd successfully concealed my intentions from him and surely now he'd stop me? He was right, tomorrow I was setting out for the Holy Fires of Pamlakar — not exactly to betray Bem and deprive him of the mortal human flesh he craved, but to try to save my sanity.

"You must do what your heart tells you to, Emma," he continued, roughly separating my thighs. "If I prevented you from going you wouldn't love me and I can't imagine a life where you do not love me." Pushing me back gently against the cushions, he began fondling my bare shoulders. "The loss of your love and this warm, woman's human body is the one thing I couldn't stand. But, the Aamir, that holy commander of spirits will say one thing and one thing only when you tell him your fear at the loss of your humanness. He'll say the only cure is to rid yourself of me, consign me to the flames of transformation and thus free Shankar's soul. Throw me to the fire, darling, then all you'll have is a dull glow to light your darkness, a feeble flickering reminder. It's true you'll still have that feeble placid soul and be able to take it out of Pandora's Box like a pet and touch and caress it. However, this demon cock, full of demon fire and able to give such blissful ecstasy, will be gone."

I sunk into deep orgasmic bliss, searing tendrils of energy wriggling up my legs and licking around my labia. Why did I cling to the futile hope that there might be an answer and I could have both worlds? Gliding down between my knees, he began foraging, his smooth tongue pistoning back and forth between my flaccid dripping lips and in response I raised my hips and rocked into him. My hands, toes, every inch of my flesh was quivering and burning with passion. The world of the jinn was inside me and on my skin and it burned me up with an orgasmic fire, drawn from the core of a burning celestial star. In that moment, I knew that Bem was my addiction and I belonged to him as much as he belonged to me — both of us prisoners of our wicked impulses, our eternal love.

Running my hands across his dewy burnished skin, I was trapped in a tantalising half trance, anticipating the slick burning fire of a demon's touch. Carefully slipping the keys from around my neck, I held them tightly in my hand. Always I was aware of how they burned Bem's tender flesh, but I must be careful to replace them. Once again I surrendered to his fingers enticing me. He wet my thighs with his issue and I spread myself over him, my bracelets jingling, my lips coming down to stroke the slippery invader. I bit his cock gently with my teeth, feeling him arch his hips and clench his fists, his thumb pressing down on my clit. His caress continued to travel over me in a blissful medley of sensations while he massaged my sex with his thumb and finger, peeling aside the glistening roseate folds and stroking them. Finding my secret places, he worked them and with a jolt I realised he was massaging the length of my clit stem, his fingers flickering points of needle pleasure. Soon, the orgasm tore through me, expanding in ripples, exploding deep inside me, the muscles of my womb contracting around finger and cock, my body pulsing as not one but a million explosions detonated all over me.

That night as I tossed and turned and Bem held me tightly in his devil's embrace, I experienced tortured dreams of the first days when Shankar was a mortal.

Chapter Six

Part Two

The Past

I'd dispensed with my hat so my hair flowed down around my shoulders in a golden cascade. Freed now of my mother's two ivory combs, it was the colour of sunlight, the perfect foil as Granny Rowena used to tell me, for my high Russian cheekbones and startling eyes.

David Hasgarth's expression lit up when he spotted me across the dining room of the hotel and he began waving his handkerchief.

I was still wearing black although I despised it, but the darkness of my simple bias-cut dress did everything for my sex appeal and the clean lines of the simple flowing black satin cocooned my gently curving body to perfection. Heads turned to appraise me as I stood feeling a little lost in the doorway of the Palm Court, clutching my purse and gazing around. That lunchtime, I think I was responsible for many glasses of champagne being spilt.

Obligation could be a hideous bore I thought, but since Marylyn was in Delhi and I was making one of my rare trips to see my solicitor Mr Panjari, it would have been downright rude of me not to stop in at the hotel and say hello. I adored the Palm Court and had fond memories of Granny and I going there. Granny Rowena had loved dining out. Birthdays and celebrations were the one rare occasion when even though she considered herself a recluse, she'd put on her most appealing gown and have the chauffeur drop us right outside the hotel so we could walk in, arm in arm. "They do such a splendid and graceful afternoon tea," she'd say. "You wouldn't have finer at the Ritz."

Now, after swiftly glancing about myself, I set forth across the large ocean of floor towards the Pennington's — Marylyn with her browbeaten covert looks, the two men David, and Marylyn's husband Henry, and Henry's mother, the formidable German Mrs Fassbender, a huge ship of a woman dressed in a flowing gown and sporting a hat of extravagant feathers and who was at that moment extracting her eyeglasses from her purse.

I was an excellent actress and good thing too, because the smile pasted to my lips was not at all genuine. Smiling didn't come naturally to me since I felt I was an observer and not fully participating in what was going on around me. Indeed, the feeling I had about life was that I was in possession of a ticket on a through train taking me to a much more interesting destination.

The occupants of the table looked up at me admiringly, especially the men.

"Well, dear Emma, what a surprise, we didn't expect to see you here although Marylyn said you might find the time," Mrs Fassbender commented, her gaze drifting over my gown and down to my stockings and neat shoes. "I never did know a woman carry off black so well apart from Mrs Ippenheimer, who looked glorious in black."

I glanced around the table. The two women nodded at one another and Mrs Fassbender adjusted her eyeglass so she could better appraise me. "Goodness, dear, what a dreadful time you've had. It was such a shock losing your grandmother that quickly."

Marylyn clutched Mrs Fassbender's arm in warning.

"Yes," I said. "Granny's death was very hard but she was so ill it really was the best thing, and I'm recovering quite well, thank you."

Dabbing at his lips with his napkin, David gazed at me compassionately. "Don't let's be like the inquisition for poor Emma," he said. "She doesn't want to dwell on things. Let's talk of lighter things, like how utterly gorgeous she looks, just like a movie star."

"But your grandmother died a considerable while ago now, though," Mrs Fassbender carried on remorselessly. "I'd have thought you'd be out of the mourning and into something more colourful?"

The table fell into an uncomfortable silence until Marylyn, suddenly realising how rude she must appear, stood and drew over a chair from another table. "You must sit down, Emma."

After a few minutes David leaned across the table. "So, why are you here then?"

"Legal things actually," I replied, gazing into his eyes, framed not pleasantly by his insipid blond eyelashes. "I have to see Mr Panjari to enquire about one or two things and adjust my will, then I thought why not be decadent and spend a day or two here at the Chandrapoor hotel, spoiling myself and perhaps seeing Mr Shrim to have my astrological chart done."

"The Chandrapoor hotel, eh?" Henry commented. "Why would you do that? It's far from seemly a woman staying at an international hotel on her own, and it'll cost you a pretty penny too, young lady."

"She has the money I think," David said, sitting back amused. "She is, after all, a woman of means now, aren't you, Emma?"

Mrs Fassbender was staring at me with a glint in her eyes. "Mr Shrim did you say? But, dear, he's a heathen. If I recall, he gave a talk at Mrs Kirkbride's and scandalised everyone. I recollect the horrible little man very well. He's a devil worshipper and he talks no end of nonsense causing me to have nightmares for months. Why" — she sipped her tea — "the man's a self-confessed seer who can see his own mortality and the end of the world."

"I think that's enough of this ridiculous talk," David interposed. "He's the same as a great many Indians that's all, much more spiritually inclined than us westerners, a guru and fairly harmless. To be truthful" — he turned to me, squeezing my hand reassuringly — "I find him pleasant and rather amusing."

Marylyn stared at Mrs Fassbender with a recriminating expression before turning to me. "What an unfriendly lot you must think us, Emma. I apologise, but I'm speaking for us all when I say, it's only because we care so much about you and we haven't seen you in ages."

The wall of faces, belonging to my friends, stared at me with some degree of expectancy. I realised that I was being speculated over and gossiped about madly. I could intuit the whispers. A single, wealthy and supposedly alluring heiress, why was it I shunned men — even the most perfect, kindest gentleman?

Why? Because, of course, I was like the rest of my crazy family, unstable and possessed of strange whimsies and predilections. This made me fascinating to the male sex but something of a novelty.

"You will have some afternoon tea, won't you?" Marylyn enquired. "There's buckets of it, they always give generous portions here. I'll have someone go and fetch an extra teacup."

"It doesn't matter," I said quietly, aware of David's dancing gaze. "I can't stay long."

"You must. You've nothing else to do and for the life of me I can't think why you'd be in a hurry to get back to Langhousa. It horrifies me to think of you rattling around that huge creepy bungalow all on your own."

"Oh, Langhousa's not creepy at all, how can you say that? I love it," I said, fluffing out my skirt. "I can never wait to escape the dust and heat of the city and get back there."

Langhousa had been in my family for several generations. It was a bungalow in the plantation style possessing neat gardens brimming with exotic plants and full of the naughty monkeys I adored and who were my continual companions, although Anya hated them, and was continually chasing them with her broom. Langhousa had been built by the colonel many years ago amongst the verdancy of the foothills. The colonel had fallen in love with India when he'd first set foot on its shores, but he'd particularly loved this little enclave with its jungles full of birds, its lush valleys and gently climbing terraces. He'd also seen something mystical about it and that same mysticism had entranced his wife. The distant holy peaks, the home of the gods, capped in snow even in the summer months had been her favourite thing to muse upon when she'd been reading or doing her embroidery.

Sometimes the clouds hung over the terraces in big fluffy cotton balls and she had then said it was similar to living in Heaven.

To please his wife, the colonel had had large windows placed at angles so she could see the many aspects the house afforded. Inside there were tall, airy rooms, and on the one side the jungle almost came up the house in such overwhelming abundance she had said she had felt like a forest nymph.

My bedroom was a pleasant one at the back of the property from where I could see the startling green canopy of the jungle moving in slow undulations up the hillside. The leaves of the tea bushes shone and above the distant mountains the tattered clouds often seemed to be creeping down through the tea plants, twisted like garlands on a Christmas tree. When Granny Rowena had inherited it, she had fashioned incredible gardens, and quite by accident, had stumbled upon the path down through the jungle leading to one of the tributaries of the holy river. The stream and its pool had been hidden by thick foliage but were in fact only a few steps away from the summer house. Granny, who'd originally come from Ireland, had said it was the home of the fey, or as they were called here in India, the notorious and mischievous jinn. Rowena and I would sit for hours with her holding my arm, her eyes had been bright with excitement whilst we had watched the magical shapes in the shifting patterns of the leaves and waters. Even Anya said it was a special place. Once there had been a temple by the pool but now there were only a few stones left and it was here Anya left offerings to the gods of fruit and flowers and tiny Hindu statues. The most interesting thing was the tiny cave above the pool leading into the hillside. One day

Rowena's Jack Russell terrier, Spark, had vanished down the cave and re-emerged a long way away with his tail between his legs and a woebegone expression on his face. He'd never gone back there afterwards, Rowena insisting this was because the caves were the home of the bad jinn. Grandfather, who did not believe in jinn, said it was more likely to be the homes of snakes or mongooses.

I was snapped out of my reverie by an elegant waiter who'd bought an extra teacup and plate and I now sipped fine Ceylon tea whilst enduring the chit chat and the voices in the large stately room with its dark furniture and proliferation of palms. Everyone was watching me out of the corners of their eyes, the men with predatory looks, the women a mixture of admiration and jealousy.

It was natural for me, when I felt under threat, to edge closer to that other place of spirit. I did this now, blinking once or twice and smiling at the marvel of it whilst the familiar curtain gradually descended over my consciousness. During these absences I slipped into a state of transcendental bliss, my body humming with the promise of delectations to come. The Spence women had all been prone to these intermittent fancies, and Rowena, who'd suffered from them notoriously, had called them 'the whisper', the result of an occult hiccup. When they occurred she simply went to bed in a dark room and revelled in a period of astral travelling. I liked to think of it as passing through a permeable door into a spirit world resembling an exact facsimile of the mortal one. Sometimes spirit threw the door wide open like they were doing today and when they did, something extraordinary happened. The Chandrapoor tearooms seemed exactly the same and yet changed, the colours intensely bright and the air so highly spirit-charged that my skin prickled as ghostly forms flitted between the tables and elegantly took tea amongst their mortal sisters and brothers, raising their cups and hats to me and even dancing, whilst the mortals carried on obliviously and totally unaware of them.

I drifted for a while, the occasional etheric guide rope pulling me a little bit closer to that tantalising other place. How lucky I was, I thought, adding more sugar to my cup.

"Good gracious, look, it's Shankar," Marylyn said suddenly, nudging me and directing my attention towards the door through which Shankar, carrying an enormous package under his arm, had just strolled. "You remember him, don't you, Emma?"

Yes, I remembered him. In fact, I had carnal knowledge of him. Unknown to my fellow diners, the interconnecting threads of my soul and Shankar's had become entwined a second time, about a month before at the hospital in Dakir where there had been a dreadful outbreak of malaria and I had decided to attend for a week or so as a volunteer. He'd been leaning over a bed attending to a patient and I hadn't been able to see much of him other than his white slightly crumpled coat, an old stethoscope and the angular beauty of his cheekbones.

The Dakir hospital had once been an old nunnery and the rooms were tall and cooled by ceiling fans, the large shuttered windows opening out onto a peaceful square courtyard. He had known I was there—I had noticed it in the slight stiffening of his body and the way he had moistened his lips and had hesitated. When he had turned around he had been excessively beautiful for a man. His skin was the colour of dark honey and his eyes large and luminous.

He'd asked to meet me for tea at the Formentosa hotel and we'd sat in the tea rooms, his hand in mine, his thumb stroking gently back and forth over my skin, seducing me simply with that rhythmic touch. I knew I was in love.

"We'll have to employ subterfuge," he'd said. "Are you in Delhi frequently, Miss Spence?"

"Yes. Fairly often. There's always some pretext to do with the house, or supplies or even social engagements." I'd been sipping tea and watching him with a smile on my lips. "Are you afraid of compromising my reputation Mr Maravar?"

His dark eyes had drilled into mine. "Of course, of course. I must not be seen to compromise a young white lady's fine standing and I think I already did that once at the hotel if you remember?" He had winked at me. "Indian men and rich heiresses must not be seen together, it would make things too difficult for you. But I must see you. We must take a room and begin, I think, to explore this possibility since fate has this habit of pushing us together."

"Yes," I'd agreed. "A nice room. Somewhere for an affair, not the kind of room a dirty whore would book."

"Definitely not." He had squeezed my hand. "I'm an Oxford educated man, so it has to be a nice hotel, not the kind of hotel for a dirty assignation. A hotel like this, for example. Somewhere stylish and far enough away from the hospital."

"Yes, this would be the perfect hotel," I'd commented, gazing around myself. At that precise moment, I had watched a movie star enter the foyer, glance around and pull off her long gloves. Evidently, by her covert demeanour, she was in the throes of some assignation.

The Formentosa dated back to The Raj. It was a romantic hotel and perfect for us since it was a reasonable distance from the hospital and few of my friends ever frequented it. It was also relaxing, with staff who knew the value of decorum and style, and because of that, was a frequent haunt of film stars, diplomats and the decadent idle rich.

We agreed to meet the following Wednesday.

Now, watching him stroll through the lounge with women gazing at him and pausing in the middle of conversation, their forks raised, my pulse raced.

"He's like a god, isn't he? God Shankar," Marylyn added, putting her mouth close to my ear. "There's one for you, darling. They say he has exotic and unorthodox tastes. Wouldn't you be tempted to fuck him?"

"Don't be so disgusting," I mumbled under my breath, smiling brightly.

"The Indian doctor, Mr Maravar's son?" Mrs Fassbender said with a grimace. "My goodness, he strikes a figure, doesn't he? So debased with it, though, and a loose cannon by all accounts. They say he talks about nothing but sex and mysticism. Another one of those wayward mystics like Mr Shrim."

On glancing at Marylyn, I saw that her look was fierce.

"We really shouldn't encourage him," the elderly lady continued. "He's hardly the kind of man you should be introducing Emma to."

Marylyn bobbed her head. "He's nothing like Mr Shrim, and come along, it's just gossip. An eligible man who doesn't date is bound to invite speculation, and dear Mrs Fassbender, he's a respected Indian mystic, after all. He gives talks at the Chandrapoor Metaphysical Society."

I felt like the breath had been sucked from my body. How dare he? Had he known I'd be here? Yes, he must have done. Perhaps I'd mentioned it or possibly my friend Merkel had mentioned something at the hospital.

Shankar approached the table, his stare met mine and tantalising subterfuge danced between us. He excited me immensely. He was the first mortal man who ever had. In fact, I was charmed and enthralled by a man not of my caste or class but whose view of the spiritual had elevated me to those orgasmic heights I thought I'd never achieve with a mortal. This was because Shankar was different to other men. He was like me and shared my unique view of the world — both of us aspiring to be more than mortal.

His gaze flickered around the table, reserving a special look for me. It was wonderful being plunged into this fantastical scenario and added a spicy garnish to my life. On the one hand I could envisage myself an actress in a well-rehearsed play, on the other we were spies working for different government agencies, having carnal knowledge of one another and meeting by accident in public.

"Dear Shankar, are you well?" Marylyn asked, directing a black look at the large hessian covered package.

He laughed. "Why, don't you expect me to be?"

Marylyn was now shifting in her chair. "Come and join us. Henry, move along and make room and let them draw up another chair for Maravar's son."

I quivered in anticipation while his fingers stroked his chin. I had carnal knowledge of those hands, and my cheeks felt so hot someone was bound to notice.

"Perhaps five minutes," he said in almost flawless English, sitting down beside me, the sleeve of his fine-tailored suit brushing my bare arm and making me vibrate like a piano wire.

"Miss Spence, isn't it?" He beamed at me lewdly. "Do you mind if I place this under your chair?"

Marylyn grinned cynically. "Really, Shankar, I've seen that before, it's the box, isn't it? Why do you insist on carrying that thing with you everywhere you go? Do you never leave it at home? I'm sure Henry could persuade Mr Collins at the bank to provide you with a strong box."

Shankar winked at me. Bending down he pushed the box under my chair and, squeezing my ankle, sent a delicious pulse up my spine. "Well, my dear Mrs Pennington, that's certainly kind, but it's a family heirloom and I won't let it out of my sight."

I became fascinated by two lovers who had just got up to dance. I was eyeing them greedily, jealous of the fact that they could find enjoyment in mortal love when that kind of simple, fleshy gratification left me empty. Once, I'd gone to the Lion Club in Calcutta and a man had danced with me in the same way. It had been a subtle and powerfully arousing kind of dancing, making me want to clamp my legs together. Yet the sex had only nibbled at me because I didn't feel a part of it and I'd known it would disappoint me. Shankar watched my gaze. His look seemed to say, "Wait till I get you alone, I'll wind up the gramophone and we'll dance naked."

Mrs Fassbender's lips had drawn into a thin line. "I think we can guess why you won't be parted from it. It's that tool of black magic you insist on remaining attached to, isn't it? Your father was dark enough, after all, and that box is a legend."

Shankar's hand rested on my thigh. We found tremendous strength against the outside world with a simple touch.

Marylyn turned to me, breathless with excitement. "I'm so glad you and Shankar can finally both meet. He's so dreadfully clever and Dr Frederick is amazed with him. Shankar's expertise is in tropical diseases, Emma, and he's been at the malaria hospital the other side of Delhi." She was flirting shamelessly. "And now you're back, aren't you, Shankar?"

"You're looking stunning, Miss Spence." Shankar ignored Marylyn, his eyes coming to rest on the pulse at my throat. He simmered with the dirty spark of perversity I'd come to know. There was an animalism about him that made my pulse pound as I remembered the surfing caress of lips and fingers. Every time we met to partake in pleasure at the hotel, I felt like an indulgent yet naïve whore placed in the hands of a man who could be both a bestial and indulgent devil, and yet the sweetest of transcendental tutors.

I placed my hand over his. His hand was slim, his fingers long and completely smooth with the veins close to the surface. Sometimes I danced my tongue along those life-pumping veins.

"Have some tea, Shankar?" Marylyn pressed. "And please talk to delightful Emma. We keep trying to match her with suitable men but she's so fussy." Marylyn was being teasing. She'd lit a cigarette and was posing with her elbow on the table, blowing thin curls of blue smoke from her amber holder. Mrs Fassbender stared searchingly at Shankar, two bright spots of colour on her cheeks. Doubtless she was thinking what a polished seducer he was.

"You're frowning, Miss Spence," Shankar said, shaking back his hair that hung in thick black waves to his shoulders giving him the appearance of an Indian prince.

The heat was building, the both of us keeping up the pretence of polite conversation, although he must have noticed my distraction and felt my trembling through the thin material of my dress. I gathered, like me, his mind kept drifting back to the last scenario in our hotel room. Shankar could be the smoothest of operators and I'd discovered he was a supremo at acting, not giving the slightest indication we'd ever said hello, let alone spent our time in flagrante delicto. He was irresistible to women, even charming Mrs Fassbender and the well-bred society women who were wetting their lips and flirting. A feat in itself.

I pushed my leg insistently against his. I wanted him to notice me, especially since he must recall our torrid afternoon and how he'd carnally seduced me. His tender approach, stroking the clothes from my skin and kissing the naked expanses of my fevered skin had been a thousand times more potent than if he'd ripped off my dress and we'd immediately had sex, even though, I thought with a warm flush, I'd wanted him to rip off my clothes. He was stroking upwards and had now reached my mound. Sliding his fingers under the silky fabric, he crept around my knickers, making me dig my fists into the table before he found my slit and carefully bunching the silk, pushed it inside. It was like he knew exactly where my clitoris was. Parting my legs, I allowed him to move back and forth, the fabric pleasantly abrasive. It was testimony to our sensitivities that we knew when the other orgasmed. A dilation of the pupil, a flicker of the eyelashes, we were the easiest of lovers to read.

He flashed me a look of secretive triumph before pushing his chair back. "It's so nice to see you all again and to make the acquaintance of the delectable Emma, but I have a prior engagement and I fear I'm going to be too late." Taking his watch and turning it on its fob, he shook his head. "Yes, I thought so, I'm late already."

He stood up placing his hand on my shoulder, inching his fingers under my hair and against my nape whilst he caressed my arm.

"But you hardly spoke to her and she's so incredible," Marylyn said, looking at him suspiciously. "You should ask to see her again, Shankar, she evidently likes you. Look at that flush in her cheeks."

"Marylyn!" Mrs Fassbender squealed. "Don't you think you're taking your matchmaking too far?"

"We should also leave, as a matter of fact." Henry was pulling out Marylyn's chair. "Let's make a move and we can stroll out together."

Shankar walked close by me, his arm brushing mine. I knew he was watching me out of the corner of his eye.

"Look," he whispered. "I know Rowena's dead but you can't hide behind those mourning clothes forever. I think I ought to buy you a sari or something. You need to dress brighter. You're always in black with those ridiculous stockings. You must take them off. A woman has to breathe anyway. Yes, take them off and be yourself, Emma, be free, feel the sand between your toes, the grass under your feet, sense life and immerse yourself in it." His glance was intense. "Go barefoot, let me give you lessons in sybaritism."

I felt giddy with suspense. "Shankar, how dare you. Sybaritism indeed?"

"Well it's true. I'll bring you the sari and I'll dress you myself. I have to say it would give me a great deal of pleasure. I see enough of the dark. I want to be reminded of life."

"So, you want me to be like a peacock?"

"Hush," he said, pressing his finger to his lip. "You're talking too loudly and everyone will hear."

I couldn't believe we were having this conversation on the steps of the hotel. I felt his fingers close over mine, squeezing a scrap of paper in my palm. *Gracious me!* How thrilling this secret little accord was. Later I'd open it and of course it would be the date of our next assignation. Oh, how easily I recalled the first one, and each subsequent encounter only became more thrilling.

Chapter Seven

For our first meeting at the hotel I was much too early.

I fumbled with the key in the lock and opened the door. Then, unfastening my jacket and letting it slide from my shoulders, I strolled over to the window to look through the shutters at the view of the courtyard with its palms and large fountain. The room was more like an elegant suite with marble and brass fittings and a tastefully turned down bed with satin sheets and I loved it. I sat playing with the buttons of my dress wondering if this would be a purely sexual encounter and if I ought to take off my travelling dress and change into the loose robe I'd selected for the purpose. Instead I laid down and, after kicking off my shoes, promptly fell asleep only to be woken by Shankar's knock at the door shortly after.

He wandered into the room and promptly bent down to kiss my hand. He was dressed in a light linen suit and carrying a fedora, and he had the box under his arm that he then put on top of the table. I didn't feel at all nervous when he placed his hands on my shoulders and moved his practiced fingers over my skin in small circles, before resting his lips there, his touch burning.

"God, you're lovely and so different to all the others I've met, but it's even more than that. I knew it that first instant I saw you in the market."

"Different how?"

He put his hat on the table and loosened his buttons, then he kissed me hard on the lips. "Oh, I know all about you, Miss Emma Spence, and you're not like other women, are you? The women in your family are infamous sex-crazed fiends and you have a rather fascinating history. You see, I asked Merkel and she told me about your quaint talents, your intense empathy and spiritual desire, and she was quite right. I could already feel your aura when you walked into the hospital. Later, I watched you rolling bandages and you were bad at it, but you were very good at connecting spiritually with the patients." He'd taken his hand away and was loosening his cuffs and strolling over to a table where a bottle of champagne was waiting in a cooler.

"So, you know about the curse of the mad Spence women, do you?" I rested back on my hands. "Do you check out all your prospective lovers, Doctor?"

"I'd be mad not to. I meet nothing but vapid airheads at the medical conferences I go to and I won't waste my time." He glanced out of the window, hands in his pockets, a slow smile creeping over his face. "I'm as infamous as you, Miss Spence, or so it seems. I only date interesting women who have a broader view on the world. You see, I'm a deeply spiritual man and I can't see any attraction in a woman I can't interact with on a deeper level and who, well"—he was turning towards me — "seems to possess an interesting view on sex."

I was playing with my necklace. I couldn't deny the sizzling attraction when I took in his fine erect body and his slim muscular shoulders.

"I saw you before the incident in the market. It was at Mrs Carruther's séance, a year or so ago and you were with your delightful grandmother. I looked at you and I thought what a superb woman, so much oozing sex but amazingly an aura about you too, like you were floating and not entirely of this world."

"So you don't think I'm a crazy eccentric then?"

"God, what's an eccentric? It's just another word for different. You ought to hear what they call me. Yes, yes, I realise I'm a brilliant doctor. However, no doubt you've heard the dark whispers about me. My forebears, that is, all the men of my family right back to Nehru Maravar, were demon-catchers or as us Indian's would say, jinn-catchers. There are many splendid legends about Nehru. Nehru tracked demon jinn, like hunters track man killing tigers, the evilest, wiliest spirits other hunters couldn't catch. The lords of the jinn."

What a fascinating snippet of occult information. I sat up straighter. My heart was pounding and I could hardly believe my ears. "My goodness, it sort of makes Granny look rather mundane."

Pouring a glass of champagne, he then drained it thirstily and came and sat down beside me, taking my hand and kissing it. "Dear Emma, I think you never expected to meet a bona fide demon hunter, did you?"

"Not exactly." I was mesmerised. "There again, I was brought up to understand there are many worlds, Shankar, and since I can see and walk within them I know they're true." Touching my throat self-consciously, I felt myself blushing. "It seems like we're two enigmas but I'm afraid I can probably beat you in the scandal stakes. Having researched me, you already know I come from a family of mad women who see and talk to spirits and walk in their world. Besides, there's the other thing, and you can't possibly imagine how incredibly filthy some of those tales are."

"Ah, the other thing." He nodded, laughing softly. "You mean the Spence women's fatal sex appeal? The fact you come from that long line of sexual fiends I just mentioned." He was holding my hand and sensually smoothing his thumb across my palm. "Yes, I know about that and I have to say I find it an attractive trait being a sex being myself. Yes, the hysterical beautiful Spence women are caught between worlds, aren't they? Trapped in this vapid mortal life it seems they're cursed and torn in two, eating men up and spitting them out. Now, why do you think they have such insatiable appetites, Emma? Why do you think woman—that soft, gentle and spiritual creature—should become such a flesh-devouring, erotic monster?"

I peered at him, shaking my head. I felt in turmoil. "Well, I don't know, I suppose because mortal flesh doesn't satisfy them."

"Quite right. Being able to walk in the spirit world, they've developed a taste for spirit sex and no mortal man can now please them. Aimless souls and sad angels, they therefore drift, tangled up so much in their fantastical cravings, they eventually go mad. It's sad." He kissed my hand. "Very sad indeed, but you, my dear Emma, are not going to go insane."

I shivered, my hands feeling suddenly cold. He chafed them and held them to his lips before separating each of my fingers and sliding them one by one into his mouth, dancing his tongue around them. I should have withdrawn them, of course, there was something shocking about so intimate a gesture, but I couldn't, I didn't want to. The sensation was taking me to a warm salacious place and I felt a ripple pass through me. It was a sweet moment of surrender and more fascinating than actual sex. I was soon to learn that this foreplay, this licking and sucking and circling towards orgasm only made the later sex more intense.

"I know exactly what you want, Emma, and it doesn't come from this world. You seek a divine spiritual spark, a divine spiritual love. All your kind do. But, you especially, because you are my darling..." Stroking my cheek, he hesitated. "You're very special indeed. You need a man who understands the pleasure of both flesh and spirit. I adore you, Emma. I realise it sounds insane — however, I knew the moment I first laid eyes on you, you were the one I'd been searching for all my life."

He drew me against him, stroking my hair and I was speechless. The air vibrated with mysterious and invisible energies that seemed to reach out to touch me in moist dark places — between my legs and on the tips of my sensitive nipples. He was carefully loosening my buttons now, his fingers pushing aside the fabric so he could see the dark, tight nubs. "You're a mortal body clothed in spirit, Emma, and no man has ever satisfied you. They want to possess you, stick their cocks in you..." He was circling my exposed nipple with his finger — then, leaning over and with the lightest of touches, he flicked out his tongue to touch the rigid tip. "But, they don't know how to take you to that place, that place of spiritual ecstasy only spiritual men know about. That's what you crave, isn't it, Emma?"

"Kiss me," I teased, opening my mouth a fraction and wetting my lips. "Kiss me, Shankar." My heart pounding, I grasped his hair, pulling his lips down to mine, thrusting my tongue greedily against his.

He sat up, stripping his shirt from his shoulders. "I'm going to get to know you. I want to know your soul, Emma."

For the first time in ages I was aching to be penetrated. Shankar insinuated his hands under my clothes, stroking my wet patch. I held my breath, surprised at the thirsty way my body was responding. He tantalised me by fiddling with the edging of my French silk knickers and by the time he ran his finger along my slit I was already shuddering in orgasm.

"You'll hear stories about me but don't be hurt by them," he whispered in my ear. "You see the rumours are true in a way. Women seem to find me a thrilling proposition since I'm a doctor and I've taken dozens of pretty women out to the theatre or dinner. But, it never went beyond a kiss. I never fucked them, Emma. Now, I'm going to ask you something. Take your clothes off."

I stiffened like a lightning rod, catching my breath and pushing him away with my hand. "What here, all of them? What an outlandish proposition."

"No, darling, not an outlandish proposition. We're attracted to one another in much more than a mortal fashion, so why should we waste any time? And look at you, you're as wet as I am..." His hand dropped to his belt buckle.

"You're incorrigible." I laughed, but I was also turned on by the prospect. I fiddled with the rest of my dress buttons before standing up, I shimmied it all the way down, letting it fall from one shoulder and pool around my feet.

Shankar got up, wandering into the en suite. I felt strangled at the sight of him, he was so lovely, so desirable and the thought of so much physical temptation was overwhelming. He finished slipping off his shirt, and stepping out of his trousers with his back to me he bent over, regulated the taps and added a bottle of the fine-scented bath oils the hotel had provided. His skin was like satin, each muscle honed, the curve of his spine running down to his muscular yet smoothly rounded, highly lifted butt. It was then something wet exploded inside me and I couldn't help myself. I took off my flimsy undergarments and walked naked into the bathroom. I stood behind him, twining my arms around his neck, kissing his nape where the damp dark hair curled against his skin.

"Miss Spence, you truly are wanton." He turned me around and, caressing me, he helped me step in the bath before drawing me down into the scented water. "I intend to fuck you in every mortal way I possibly can, and next we'll get to work on your mind. I'll take you there, on that slow climb to Nirvana, I promise you." He drew me closer, running his hand down my spine and into my crack. The pressure of his finger and the warm water was surprisingly good and I pressed closer, aware that I was even wetter. He soaped me all over as I lay against his hard cock, his hands arousing, making smooth, slick circles over my skin until I couldn't bear it anymore. Getting up and sitting on the edge of the bath, I made him kneel, opening my legs wide so he could look at the place between them.

"I expect you see a lot of cunts, doctor?"

"Yes, Emma." He teased aside my fleshy lips. "However, not like yours. I could come out with lots of romantic flowery words about your cunt but doubtless mortal man has said them often enough."

I combed his hair with my hands, my long tresses falling loose of their pins and cascading down my neck. "Hah," I cried, biting my lip while he felt carefully around my slick walls.

After a moment or two of stroking, I wanted to push against him, thrust him high up inside me so I could satisfy myself, but Shankar had other ideas and he touched my clit with his thumb while moving his finger in and out. Before I knew what he was doing, he was spreading a towel on the floor and before lifting me gently, he laid me down. I was entirely bemused but pulsing with excitement. He placed a hand on my mound whilst with the other, he crooked his finger and, stretching high inside me, found the sacred seed, my place of intense pleasure and pressed it hard. No man had ever touched me there and I ground my teeth, the satisfaction surpassing anything I'd anticipated. Then he began to move his digit in lots of different ways until, clutching his hand, I held him there, my womb contracting around him. Afterwards, he sat me in the bath again and soaped me gently with his hands, taking time to touch me everywhere, before towelling me dry and dusting me with powder between my legs, we wandered over to the bed and laid down together.

It was evening and I felt drowsy. He was still caressing me, fingering my nipples and my cunt, and I moved in a warm pool of concentric delight. The sun was a huge orange ball outside and just beyond the gate into the courtyard we could hear the cars drawing up outside the hotel and discharging their guests, who had been out shopping or doing business. Soon another battalion of cars would come to fetch those in their finery who would be going out to dine or to the theatre.

Stretching my arms above my head, I felt him roll onto me and he began eating me slowly from head to toe, licking and sucking before he opened my legs again, holding them wide this time and gently biting my sex whilst diving his tongue in and out. It was even better than his finger and I orgasmed several times until my body felt light and soaring.

* * * *

He didn't fuck me properly for ages, not that it mattered since the heightened suspense of sexual entanglement was making me even hotter. Shankar was everything I'd ever desired in a lover, he was both romantic and seductive and searching for that most elusive of things—spiritual bliss. He brought me lovely books of Indian poetry, or daring and unusual ones on tantric and mystical sex, and we playfully teased each other, testing the boundaries of our pleasure and driving one another crazy with our fingers and tongues. Then one day he brought me an obscure volume on Indian folklore written by the dark magician Bodekar. It was about demon love and those demon spirits called the jinn.

Chapter Eight

I knew all about the jinn, of course. I'd been brought up knowing about these intriguing spirits who scared the superstitious Indian servants. But the book Shankar had given me focused on a particular shaitan who worked with the elements to spin his enticing magic. The allure of these dark jinn, the sexy and ancient raw elemental beings who drew their power from the forces of the natural world, excited and intrigued me. Often, like now, I found myself drawn back into recollections of my young best friend Marion O'Keefe and the intriguing conversations we'd had about Marion's experiences of demon love that she'd assured me at the time were true and had come to fascinate me.

According to Marion, who'd believed in it wholeheartedly, this elemental sex was something of particular interest to women and carried them away in spiritual ecstasy. Marion had been like me and Serena—she'd been born being able to see into the spirit world and she'd been obsessed with spirits. I'd met Marion at a metaphysical meeting at one of the

Chandrapoor women's houses and had instantly been enthralled by a woman who exuded darkness, frequently practiced spells from a book of dark magic and conjured demons. Marion had gone into raptures over demon love and had said no mortal man could do what a demon could do. Breathlessly she'd spun her explicit tale, explaining that she loved them ardently, shared her bed with them — in fact, was sharing her bed with one despicable character right now. *How unbelievable — but also how tantalising.* I had shivered at the thought of it and become filled with jealousy and illicit longing.

"You want to find one for yourself," Marion had enthused. "Don't even bother with a mortal man, it's a waste of time. All they want is a quick body fuck. They're not interested in your mind, not interested in..." For a moment her eyes had gone cloudy and she'd run her hands over her body. "Not interested in setting you alight, in giving you endless joy, in fucking your mind and soul."

Marion had married a diplomat, an older lenient man who'd indulged her, but she still shared her bed with the demon who she said took her to the heights of orgasmic ecstasy her husband never could. "Well, dear, he can touch me in all those places men find so hard to locate and don't know what to do with. You know the ecstasy spot and other places inside, deep down in the womb. You do understand, don't you?" She'd had a devilish look about her, her eyes glistening.

Lately our sharing of two worlds had been drawing us closer and during the recounting of her daring exploits, Marion's tales had been becoming sinister and more detailed. The demon seemed to have chained her within a dependent sexual cycle and she was at his beck and call. Besides which, she'd been changing. Everyone thought it was down to her marriage, but Marion had been becoming more and more secretive and seemed to be suffering from constant fevers and passionate outpourings.

"It's a woman's thing," her friend Harriet had said. "Women are prone to illusion. She'll soon get over it when she has a child."

One day Marion became beset by what a lot of the Chandrapoor women called the Chandrapoor malaise and she'd taken to her bed, necessitating a visit from me. The O'Keefes haad lived in a large house on the outskirts of Delhi. The house had not been as grand as Langhousa but was very pretty and decorated in the Victorian style with lots of heavy English furniture. Marion had seemed strange when she'd come into the parlour. She'd been dressed in a thin muslin gown and her sorrowful brown eyes seemed unusually bright beneath her tight curly black hair.

"I'm so glad you came," she'd said. "I didn't think you would."

"They're all talking about your marriage," I replied. "They're saying your behaviour's peculiar and that you might be having an affair." I'd been intrigued by the rumours I'd heard lately about Marion.

Marion stared hard at me, two vertical frown lines deepening on her brow. "Is that why you're here? You've heard the rumours and now you want to come and see for yourself how crazy I've become, see if I'm becoming like poor Serena? Well, she was different. You know she was. Actresses are generally delusional."

"Don't be silly."

It had been exceedingly quiet with only the ticking of the clock. Marion had sat with her hands folded, staring straight ahead of her looking rather thoughtful. After a while she'd looked up. "Dear Emma, you've no idea what it is to be married, you really don't. It's a great hardship, especially when your husband's such a prude and...well, you know... I do so enjoy sex, but exciting sex and he won't give it to me. In fact, he won't even talk about it."

"You don't love him, is that it?" I asked, leaning forward.

"How silly. Naturally, I love him in a manner of speaking, but you see I had to marry him, it was expected of me. Then, quite by chance I happened to meet someone else. I didn't mean for it to happen, it just did."

"So, they're right, you are having an affair?" I'd persisted.

Marion had sprung to her feet and come and sat down beside me, her fingers digging in my arm. "Darling, please, please don't say anything, will you? It's not like you think, and I've so been dying to tell you but dared not."

I'd been staring closely at her. I'd never seen Marion so flustered, so pink and feverish, with her eyes glowing like coals and a thin line of perspiration marking her upper lip.

"It's up to you whether you tell me or not," I'd said circumspectly. "However, because we're such good friends, I'm rather hoping you will."

Marion was chewing her lips and when I'd glanced down, I'd seen her fingers were trembling.

"Darling." She'd placed her hand in mine. "It's eating away at me and driving me crazy. There's no one else I can talk to. I mentioned it to Mother and she sent for Dr Brightstone immediately and he threatened to give me laudanum, but I'm not out of my mind, I'm not, truly."

"No, I'm sure you're not," I'd replied, becoming more and more fascinated.

"It isn't like it is in the books," Marion had said after a moment. "You go into sex thinking it will be a certain way, but it's nothing like that. That vision of sex you and I have, darling, that spiritual climb to bliss. Well, in mortal life it simply doesn't exist. He sticks his thing in and before you realise it, it's over. It's carnal and I find it disgusting and there's none of that exquisite delight, that shaking female excitement one expects. You do understand what I mean, don't you, Emma? Why" — she'd shaken her head — "I was left feeling so deprived after sex, the only way I could ever achieve that shaking excitement was to make it happen myself and I did countless times." Her voice had been rising higher, becoming strident and more demanding. "You must have done it yourself. You must have touched your thing and experimented just to see how it was. I can do it myself, however, it hardly ever happens with a man."

"Yes, yes, Marion, I do understand, but please calm down and be quiet, you don't want the servants to overhear, do you?" I'd been holding her hands tightly.

Marion peered at the carpet. She was biting her lip savagely. "I did a naughty thing, Emma dear. You won't be angry with me, will you?"

I shook my head and Marion, leaning closer, had dropped her voice so she could whisper in my ear, "You see, it wasn't like I made a naughty spell and brought him here, because that would have been very bad indeed. No, he was already here and I'd felt him before. But when I got married and I began to think of sex and I became frustrated by it, well, he seemed to come closer. Whenever I used to go down to the swing at the bottom of the garden, he'd push me higher and higher just to tease me. Then, one day when I was lying on my bed he came into my room and, well, I could see this tantalising smoky wraith and he was so ravishing, so handsome and intriguing that I couldn't help myself. I loosened my clothes and I offered myself. I'm not imagining it, Emma. You believe me, because you fucked the ghost, didn't you?"

"Yes, I fucked the ghost," I'd said quietly, my mind filling with recollections of my encounter at Colonel Roderick's house in Ceylon. I hadn't needed much encouragement to partake of etheric lust on that occasion, probably because I had been enthralled by the world of spectres and intrigued by the stories I'd read about ghostly possession. Laughingly the colonel had told me about a wicked sea captain who used to be a friend of the family and often used to stay there. The captain had had a devilish eye for women and had fallen under the thrall of the mistress of the house, a half-native woman called Portentia, who the owner of the plantation had married at a young age. The notion of this gallant, lusty seafaring denizen had been intriguing and I have to say when I'd been left alone in my room I'd felt the familiar prickle in the air that began to drive me crazy. I'd caressed my nipples and begun stroking them into firm points before slipping my camisole down my arms. It was at that moment I'd felt the captain's etheric arms come around me in a satisfying hug. At first I had thought I was imagining it. Then I'd heard a breathy voice in my ear. Soon the ghostly form of his hands appeared and he'd begun moving them over my body, stirring me, stopping to brutally pinch my nipples between his thumb and forefinger, before rolling them slowly back and forth. "Hello, my little virgin beauty."

"Yes, feel me, I'm a virgin," I'd breathed, guiding him to the throbbing place between my legs.

It had been incredibly erotic to see those ghostly, etheric hands continuing their journey under my silk panties and I'd groaned when he rubbed his fingers up and down my crotch, creating blossoms of dark juice against the silk. His hands had continued to cup and fondle as I'd felt something hard press between my butt cheeks, and heaven help me I surrendered. He had kicked my legs from under me, sending me sprawling onto the embroidered counterpane before he'd jerked down my silk underwear and took me from behind, his ghostly teeth nipping my neck. I was ashamed to say I'd enjoyed it and that was not the only occasion. That night, when I'd been lying in bed reading, I'd observed my candle gutter and flare, the flame turning intensely blue and becoming like one long length of elastic stretching towards the ceiling. The apparition had materialised in the corner of the room, a ghostly phantom composed of a diaphanous substance, that, undulating towards me, peeled back the bedclothes and had lain down beside me. He'd teased me for hours, starting firstly with my nipples and coaxing them to such a sustained pitch of sensitivity I'd trembled and detonated and found I'd wetted the bedsheets. Then the ghostly form had caressed my body until I was writhing with passion.

"Emma, are you listening?" Marion had grumbled, pinching my hand fiercely and snapping me back to the present. "Gracious, you go off so easily." Her had been smile was sly. "Are you dreaming about it, imagining what he would do to you?"

"Yes, yes, I suppose I am."

"Let me tell you, the sex was incredible and just like they say sex with a demon is..." Twisting her hair around and around her fingers, there had been a beatific look on her face. "He told me that demons adore and are attentive to mortal women and they have a weakness for warm flesh and blood. But he also told me they require an invitation, whether spoken or psychic. They'll fall in love with a mortal woman and follow her for months, years, even through lifetimes, biding their time and waiting for a moment of weakness until they manage to seduce you and you're theirs."

"Oh." I'd wetted my lips. My heart had been beating rapidly with excitement. "So, what you're trying to say is you're possessed by a demon. You have a demon lover?"

Marion shrugged. "Good Lord no, not possessed. I submitted, and don't look so high and mighty, Emma. What's wrong with it? I'm not hurting anyone, am I?"

I'd known enough about the spirit world to believe Marion. Her body had been vibrating like she was possessed by an otherworldly electrical force.

"I'll never ever be able to love a mortal man after this, Emma. Dark spirits are so infinitely passionate. Spirit fingers reach inside a human body and they are so enduring and patient they can bring a woman to the pinnacle of orgasm and hold her there seemingly suspended before starting all over again. You come alive and begin to burn and feel vibrant for the first time in your life." The next words had been uttered so quietly I thought I'd missed them. "I...I..." she stammered. "I even passed out when I climaxed."

"All right," I'd quipped. "And say I wanted to partake of this fleshy delight and I decided I liked this idea of a demon lover. How would I go about getting one?"

Marion had gently pinched my cheek. "I like your spirit." She'd covered her hand with her mouth and began giggling. "Did you hear that...like your spirit? I think I just made a joke." Pressing closer to me she'd whispered in my ear, "Joking apart, though. Well, he'll find you, you're so utterly irresistible and their spiritual and sex antenna seems so long." And at that moment she'd given me what seemed to be a dirty wink.

* * * *

It turned out Marion and I had soon been separated when her husband was posted back to England. I'd still written to her but apparently she'd become quiet and taciturn, doubtless because she had been separated from her spirit beau, and like so many friendships, ours gradually drifted apart.

And now I pondered, I had the next best thing to a demon lover. I was in love with the type of man I'd always dreamed of. A walker between worlds, a lover who wanted to take me to the same euphoric heights I dreamed of going to.

What wonderful afternoons Shankar and I had at the hotel. Sometimes he brought a gramophone from the hospital and we danced together naked and cheek to cheek. At other times we spent the entire day together in bed, wrapped in each other's arms while he fondled me between my legs, burying his hands deep in my thatch, sliding back and forth and around my hole and back up to my clit whilst I suffered an avalanche of butt-clenching multiple orgasms. All of a sudden life had become a delectable smorgasbord of sex, fantasy and indulgence, and of course there was the other thing. I often wondered about the other thing when, with my hand on my cheek, I watched him sleeping. I was falling in love, falling in love with a mystery of a man who had told me some things about himself, yet was still an enigma. Why, for instance, did he carry Pandora's Box with him wherever he went, even when Marylyn had kindly offered him their father's strongbox at the Calcutta bank? And why was it when I sneaked a touch of the forbidden box, it was so warm it felt like a fire was burning inside? Soon, the box began to intrigue me almost as much as the sex. There was a dark and compelling aura about it, something rendering Shankar silent and introspective and a shade angry. True, I knew it to be a spiritual compartment, an essential tool handed down through the centuries and used in his family's work as demon hunters, but he strictly forbade me to touch it, and even when he touched it himself, it was with extreme reverence, like he was afraid of waking something up, something slumbering inside.

* * * *

One day when he strolled in the room Shankar looked worried and beads of perspiration were dripping down his face and had stained his fine shirt. Placing the hessian-wrapped box on the floor, he sank down on the bed with his head in his hands.

"Whatever's happened?" I asked. "You look terrible."

"It's Ravrankar's box. Several times people have tried to steal it. Today a suspicious man followed me through the bazaar and chased me before he tried to corner me."

"Goodness, are you all right?"

"Yes, darling, but you see how it is? The box is extremely valuable. It's strong magic and that's why people try to steal it. There's a black market amongst magicians and relic hunters for these things."

"It must be important and very precious then?" I said.

"It is. The box is many hundreds of years old. It's a long story."

"Well, I think I'm about ready for that story, don't you?" I fashioned a moué. "So, what's the great mystery, don't you trust me? I'm sharing a hotel room with the most handsome man in India, a mystery man, so surely the least he can do is explain to me about the box he carries around everywhere."

His gaze embraced me, lingering for a moment on my erect nipples visible through my thin robe. "Of course you're right and yes, darling, I do trust you." Patting the pillows, he drew my head down onto his chest. "Do you know the legend of Pandora, darling? Well, it actually puts me in the mind of that."

"I know it very well. So, that's what the box is, is it, Shankar? A Pandora's Box of sinful treasure and you're like my Mercury, jealously protective of his charge but refusing to let me touch it or lift the lid."

Pressing his finger to my lips, he glared at me sternly. "There are sometimes good reasons for caution, believe me." He began stroking my shoulder. "I'll tell you what I know, Emma. Often we dismiss myths as fables, but mystics believe they're metaphors for spiritual truths, fireside stories, that are then committed to memory or written down in books. My father believed in that quaint tale, because he said the story of Pandora's Box was really a story about, the jinn box, a trap for evil spirits. These boxes are ancient and have always existed, although the earlier ones may have been simple clay sealed jars."

"Goodness, how astonishing. So you're saying the story of Pandora is true?"

"Yes, I suppose I am. But in this case the box is not tied up with a cord like Pandora's Box, it's tied up with the curious rites of magic, and the series of locks and keys and incantations devised by Ravrankar."

Resting my fist on his chest, I peered enraptured into his eyes. "Tell me more."

Shankar kissed my fingers. "In the fourteenth-century the nomad Nehru Maravar travelled across many continents. He was the greatest master of demons and jinn of his age and he was known from Constantinople to the courts of the King of England. Morning, noon and night he spent his life fasting and making rituals of purification because it was important that the master be of stoic faith and the cleanest vessel." Shankar's voice was becoming soft and sleepy and I lay there my fingers resting lightly on him, hardly daring to breathe whilst the incredible story unfolded and the familiar sounds of the Formentosa hotel drifted away. Firstly, I was transported to the hot arid desert, then the mountains, following Nehru's lonely, wandering figure through the heart of Africa.

"He was a legend, Emma, and everyone knew of him. They would call for Nehru if they had an exceedingly evil demon their magic men could not control." Shankar drew my mouth down onto his, kissing me fiercely, and I felt the lust surge. He was silent for a moment, threading my hair through his fingers. "I hardly know how to say this, darling. Although a force for good the box can be terribly evil and once, some time ago I did something I'm ashamed of." He moistened his lips. "I'm human and I've got a human's failings and because of that I'm tempted."

Sitting up, I folded my arms across my chest, feeling a quivering sense of both loathing and interest. "What, what is it?" I croaked. "Please tell me, I want to know."

After a few moments Shankar closed his eyes. "I have inherited the gifts of my forebears but I am not my forebears and a part of me is weaker than in the other Maravar sons. I don't know if it's lack of faith exactly but I seem to have a weakness for the very thing I exorcise, the jinn. I admire them, Emma, I find them fascinating and part of me feels drawn to their world and their existence. Please, darling." Grabbing my hand, he held it tightly. "Don't be afraid and please don't hate me, but that's why I fled my life in the village. I could feel myself falling into the darkness and losing my faith. When Aunt died she left me a great deal of money and I escaped. I used it to pay for a fine education in Oxford and medical school. I thought if I took myself away from the aura of India for long enough I'd be able to forget the tenebrous thread pulling me back to these dark spectres and I could cure myself of the fascination."

"I don't understand."

"Please let me finish." He held me tightly, his nails digging into my flesh. "When I went to Oxford I had to take the box. You see, I couldn't leave it. But more and more I was sure that the box or what was in the box spoke to me and made me do bad things. You see, just like Pandora's Box, a whisper drove me mad, until on one occasion, passing by and hearing this compelling voice begging me to pay attention to its message—I lifted the lid and listened and it was Bem, begging me for his freedom. He spoke to me, telling me of the ancient ways and of dark and mysterious magic. Anyway, I returned to India a qualified doctor thinking that my old life—my life of a demon hunter—would be forgotten, but as it happens, that was not the case for it seems we cannot escape our true destiny that easily. Before long the hill people once again began knocking at my door. My fate followed me. They had not forgotten who I was despite my fine voice and my fancy clothes. I was still Shankar the demon hunter, inheritor of the skills of my father."

I was frozen by the look in his eyes. "Tell me the rest of the story about this naughty Pandora's box of secrets then? Bem's evil, isn't he?"

"No, Emma, not evil in the sense you think he is. It's true Bem's a demon god, but he's also part of a great legend. You see, he was born far out in the deserts of what is now Namibia when this world was created. He was an incredible shape-shifting jinni who could transfer his spirit into the wind, the sand, a stick, a stone, a creature or a man, and like all living things he had boundless curiosity and sought constant evolution. Bem searched for his particular evolution and metamorphosis through sex and love, his spirit travelling aimlessly, until one day, while he blew across the desert, he encountered Mufasi, who was in the bush doing what naughty Mufasi did best— fucking her lover."

"And who was Mufasi?" I asked, caught up in this intriguing tale.

"Mufasi was a black princess, the daughter of a witchdoctor and by all accounts a dazzling enchantress and very agreeable to the eye. Bem thought he'd never seen a more exotic creature and when he observed their passionate encounter and saw the dirty games that Mufasi and her lover were engaged in, for the first time he felt drawn to taste mortal woman's flesh — but as a man and with a man's cock. Mufasi and her man writhed naked on the desert floor and Bem thought how glorious love looked, for surely these two tempestuous humans were in love. Even with his powers, though, Bem was tricked, for we both know, Emma, sex is easy to achieve but true love is the hardest thing to find and Mufasi did not believe in love."

I wondered how Mufasi could not believe in love and I was about to speak, but Shankar silenced me with a shake of his head.

"Listen, Emma, I haven't told you all of the story yet. The darkest of witches, Mufasi drew her power from the elemental earth and she used the power of her lovers only to enhance her sex magic, meaning she had a rabid need to fuck but only to increase her diabolical powers. When he entered her lover, she felt Bem and when Bem tasted her body she welcomed it, and his dark power together with her own, fuelled her sex magic. Bem, in his turn, felt this man's love for Mufasi, for this man had been duped and in his idiocy he was drugged by Mufasi's beauty and truly believed she loved him. Bem relished this mere taste of the thing called human love and the encounter intrigued and fascinated him even more than before, so from that day he developed a passion for tasting human flesh and obsessively he occupied body after body, continually hoping that during his mastery of the flesh he would touch true divine love again and perhaps more powerfully."

Shankar continued to hold me, kissing my hair.

"Surprisingly, he found mortal women welcomed him because he could give them what they secretly craved, the sex of legends. Bem's story became a fable etched in dark demon history since he left a trail of sex carnage. The women and men possessed by Bem acquired great sexual prowess and mastery and they became famous in their cultures for their voracious desires. However, the tale is not all good because such heinous acts gleaned from the realm of elemental spirit — where sex is raw passion and pleasure — made women aimless and greedy, thus destroying the love and attraction they had for their husbands and lovers."

I gently circled Shankar's nipples as he fanned my hair out in a curtain around my shoulders. "Tell me more. That's not the entire story, is it?"

"No, that isn't the entire story. Bem was immortal and the wind carried him all over the world to Europe and to the farthest reaches of the Orient. For the most part, it was a fleshy quest devoid of love until, that is, he came to the Far East and the court of Mabuto and the virgin daughter of the chief. His youngest daughter, Tarin was to be initiated into a holy priestess order but although she was chaste she was a highly strung woman and had the most ribald fantasies. Bem crept into her chambers, observing her while she touched herself and once again his interest was piqued but this time in a new and more powerful way. He had never known a virgin woman with such a dirty mind and this trait in Tarin confounded him so much he thought he would tease her. Tarin, who was pale and pretty and living half in the spirit world, had a soft, gracious and angelic presence about her that tormented Bem. This pure lovely creature was the exact opposite of Mufasi, and her blend of gentle virgin and burgeoning high priestess together with her curiosity regarding sexuality had Bem besotted.

He'd watch her strolling through the temple gardens transfixed with love. Yes, this heathen creature who had destroyed so many marriages and betrothals, adored her. Because Tarin did not have a human lover, how could he fuck her and thus get a taste of what he so desperately wanted? Whilst he pondered what to do he was very mischievous indeed and he vented his frustration in naughty games, terrorising the women at the wash house and curdling the milk and generally creating havoc. Plagued by her, he tried to occupy her dreams, making Tarin have bad thoughts that woke her and made her put her fingers between her legs. He then became the wind tangling her hair and headscarf and driving the raindrops in her face.

"Tarin, who was as sensitive as we are to the other world, felt all this and she intuited his presence too and it excited her. Soon, she began to wonder if she was suited to become a priestess and lead such a life, but it was already too late and how could she disappoint her family? Her doubts and hungers saw Tarin change from the sweet, biddable girl she once was into someone dark and passionate."

"It's easy to see why," I exclaimed, enchanted by the tale.

"Bem, in his turn, was now obsessed," Shankar continued. "And he was in a delirium of despair as the day of her initiation approached. He knew that once she was within the confines of the holy temple of women, Tarin would be forever lost to his powers. Following her down to the sacred pool where the virgins bathed for their purification, Bem hid behind a rock salivating with lust, and it was then that the notion struck him. A great jinn god, he had huge powers and if he could make himself a raindrop and thus caress his beloved, he could also make himself the pool itself. Bem summoned the elements and, using all the forces of magic at his disposal, he forced the jinn elemental of the water to accept his spirit form so he could become one with the watery medium and thus change his jinni body into flowing molecules that could stroke and entrap his beloved. When Tarin descended into the water and began combing her fingers through her hair, she stared in the pool and saw the ghostly image of an exceptionally handsome man who was intoxicating to her senses. It did not take Tarin long to yield to Bem's skilful fingers because she guessed who it was with her acute perception, having felt him before in the wind and rain. He coaxed her body into opening and he feathered her shivering skin with sublime dancing motions, touching her everywhere. Opening her legs she cried out, sinking beneath the water and allowing him to invade her fully, becoming one vibrating orgasm of delight.

"Tarin felt him come inside her and touch her sex, bringing her to such an apogée of ecstasy she floundered to the surface and, just making it to the bank in time, fainted. That was where her maid found her. The maid, in turn, called the king and servants who were almost hysterical that Tarin, who looked like a ghost, might die. Tarin was carried back to the palace and attended by the court physician, and reluctantly her mind came back from its flight of ecstasy to nestle in her mortal body. When she opened her eyes, though, they shone with an otherworldly light because she'd been possessed by Bem, whose liquid fingers had felt inside her, and with his magic had become her blood and essence and had taken her earthly virginity with his magic. When Tarin's father leaned over her he guessed what had happened since he'd seen such instances of possession before. It was then he called for my forebear, the legendary Nehru Maravar, who had to make a journey of many days from the East. It is said that Nehru had a mighty struggle exorcising and capturing Bem, who having now tasted divine earthly love was loathe to yield it up to the demon master."

I was so astounded by this tale I realised that I'd been holding my breath and I exhaled gently, shaking my head incredulously. How I wished I was Tarin, submitting to her passionate dark lover. "That's a long way of explaining to me about the box, Shankar, but what an amazing story."

"Yes, and that's not the end. Nehru placed Bem in the box because the box is one of only two and one of the strongest and most powerful prisons for jinn ever made. The wood comes from a special fragrant tree in the Holy Land that was blessed by Ravrankar, the great Egyptian mystic. Ravrankar was a master at these things and his magic commanded the strictest obedience from black souls. He put a virtually impregnable force field around the box so it could hold the most terrible spirits and he carved strong magic in the form of a Sanskrit spell around its sides."

"It sounds like Mr Patel's strongbox at the post office and it would take a bull elephant to get in there," I said humorously, grim realisation dawning as I gazed at the box and felt myself shiver. Suddenly, it had taken on a darkly macabre appearance. "So, this Bem's still in the box, even after all that time? How incredible!"

Shankar blinked at me and spread his hands. "Yes, and what a perilous journey he's had. For Bem should have perished when my forebears took the box to be emptied at the Holy Fires. When one attends the Holy Fires, the box is shaken so hard the spirits fall into the flames to be reborn and sent back to the world of the jinn. Bem's attachment to this earthly existence was so great, though, he spun the last feeble threads of magic he had, so he could not be shaken free, and like a monkey he clung to the walls of the box. The trouble is, though, he weakens and the longer he's in there the feebler he becomes until eventually, unless he can devise an escape, the day will arrive when with one good shake Bem will have to relinquish his hankering for mortal flesh and yield to that fiery furnace. You see, Bem's sustenance was love and sex and it's now so long since he's had what he craves, he's weak and only the palest shadow of what he was."

I felt a strong clenching fist in my belly I recognised as fear. "Surely then you can see the danger? Hasn't he been waiting for a weak spirit to possess so that he can plan his escape?"

Shankar twined his fingers through mine and shook his head tiredly. "In many ways you're right in your fear because you can't possibly imagine how strong the faith of a demon hunter must be. At the time of exorcism a demon will test your resolve, taking you close to the fires of creation and tempting you with his devilish tricks. They're such beautiful circean creatures, Emma. Once, I attempted to exorcise a female jinni with immense power and she lured me into her world. Her beauty blinded me like only a truly wicked soul can. She had a body of endless fiery delight and I'd never felt such happiness. I allowed her to seduce me. I understand what you're thinking, Emma. You think I may not be strong enough to control Bem and you're right, for my resolve is questionable and I'm drawn to the darkness. But you see we have the power of Ravrankar's box and that magic will protect us."

"And what of Bem, what thrall does he hold over you?" I asked shakily, my limbs frozen with fear. The room was silent. I felt horrified waiting for his response.

"Darling Emma." He peered at me gravely. "Bem intrigues me, he always has. In many ways he's the other half of me, the half I'm too afraid to acknowledge—the darker, mystical side I wish to indulge, but why can't two halves exist as one? My sweet, I've been tempted, tempted to conjure his presence, but I swear I never have."

By this time, I was feeling dizzy and the room was swaying vertiginously.

Shankar leant forward and cupped my chin. "Sweetheart, please don't be terrified, I would never do it. Yes, I've been tempted but I'm not a fool. Whatever happens he's safely locked in the box and there's no way he can escape. He's consigned to a life of imprisonment in that magical fortress." Shankar was squeezing my hand tightly. "Listen to me, Emma. Over the years I've come to have great respect for this creature. Born of the maelstrom of desire, all he ever sought was ecstasy through human love."

"But, you don't know what harm he could cause, Shankar. Demons are tricksters and Bem's intrigued by human sexuality. He seeks out warm human bodies and he's demonstrated to you he'll stop at nothing to cling to this world. What makes you think he doesn't want to possess you? That he can and will possess you?"

"Calm down, Emma. Whilst the box is kept locked there's no danger."

"There is danger, a great danger. He's a jinn demon." Clambering off the bed, I stood with my fists at my sides, my eyes filling with tears. "You sound like you're obsessed with this creature. No wonder you carry the box around everywhere. Do you conspire with him? Do you help him to plot his escape? Have you, in fact" — I wavered — "welcomed him into your body, and already been possessed by him? Have you been enjoying me, even while that creature, that dark spectre, has been savouring and indulging himself too?"

Shankar had leapt to his feet and was now holding me, shaking me gently by the shoulders. I tried to push him away. "Oh God, Emma, you see why I didn't tell you this before? How could you understand this when even I question it? But even if I was possessed, would it be such a bad thing? For isn't possession simply another name for cohabitation by a spirit? A spirit seeking a safe haven, a haven where it can continue to learn and thus grow towards its ultimate destiny? And the mortals Bem possessed were never taken against their will, they were curious about him, sex hungry beings, searching for sensations this world could never give them. Look at me, Emma, don't hate me. Don't you see how possession can be the best of both worlds, and aren't all of us possessed in one way or another, for what are addictions for sex and love, if not possession?"

"How can you say that?" I shook my head vehemently, biting my lip and looking away whilst shudders passed through me. "Don't you see he's a trickster and he has you believing his lies?"

"Darling Emma, he doesn't lie, and believe me when I say you have nothing to fear. I'd never do anything to endanger you. I love you and that's why I'm telling you the truth." Touching the keys he kept around his neck, he held them up. "Whilst I hold the keys, we're safe. I have dominion over him and he can't escape. A special cipher is needed to open the box and three keys have to be turned in a precise way to open it. There's no prison like this, it's truly a prison fashioned by a genius."

I was confused, since despite finding this revelation repellent I was also fascinated. "Let me take a proper look at this sinful box of secrets, then?"

"I don't think that's a good idea, Emma."

"What do you think I'm going to do? I'm not Pandora. I'm not going to let every evil in the world out of there."

For a moment he seemed to be considering something. There was doubt in his eyes, but I could tell that in his love for me, he wanted to be open and reveal this darker part of himself. Slipping his hand around my waist, he pulled me closer, kissing my mouth gently. "All right, darling, but now can you see why this box must never fall into the wrong hands?" Shankar strolled to the table. Next, he unfolded the hessian, taking out the box in its covering of black silk.

I approached it, my mouth dry and my heart pumping. Stretching out my finger, I touched the wood and instantly a shock travelled up my hand. "Ouch, what was that?" I rapidly withdrew my hand, sucking my finger.

"The box has a life force of its own. It's such a powerful magic, but you soon get used to it, see..." Shankar took my finger and began to trace it along the box's rich carvings. "It can't be opened by accident. The box is protected by its magical lock and language. Always to open it you turn the box anticlockwise."

"Are you sure you want to show me this?"

Shankar pressed my hand to his lips. "Yes, Emma. I adore you and I don't want to hide these secrets from you any longer. Only you and Vasi know about the box, but I don't trust Vasi with Bem. For certain Vasi would destroy him since he knows all about Bem Hazari and he would take him to the Holy Fires without a moment's hesitation."

"And who's Vasi?"

"You'll learn about him soon enough." Picking up his jacket, he reached inside the pocket and took out a slim book, lovingly stroking the cover. "There are three keys for the box." He took the chain containing the keys from over his head. "Here are two, but the final key's in here. This is the book of Ravrankar. Inside are the words used to summon forth and to capture dangerous spirits. You must be careful to never forget to hide the third key in the book. No demon will ever dare touch the book of Ravrankar because it feels like ice to him and it freezes his jinn spirit."

"This Ravrankar must have been a very powerful man?" I exclaimed, peering at the book, that was undoubtedly one of the most unusual I'd ever seen. It appeared to be many hundreds of years old and was bound in black leather with tooled designs on the cover. Inside, the few pages it contained were scribed in intricate Arabic lettering, each hand-painted with exquisite designs. On the one page was a painting of what seemed to be angry avenging angels, on the next a depiction, supposedly of the demons of hell. The back of the book was hollowed out and composed of false pages providing a nest for the last tiny black key.

"Before the box is opened the spell of containment must be recited, so that what is inside cannot escape. Next, the keys must be turned anticlockwise and in the right order." Shankar held up the first and larger key of the other two. "You push this key all the way in and give it a half turn. The second key fits half way and is given another half turn, and this smallest key, the key inside the book — the smallest one — you barely push in and give a full turn. It's a mechanism that has confounded mystics and prophets down through the centuries."

I felt excited. Trailing my fingers over the book of Ravrankar a burst of etheric electricity sent delicious ripples over the surface of my skin. Now the box was becoming less foreboding and more thrilling.

Shankar smiled, settling the keys around his neck and placing the book in his pocket.

I wandered to the window and Shankar came up behind me, kissing my nape and gently lifting my hair away from my neck. All of this was incredible, but I knew about the otherworld and I knew what mysteries and secrets it held.

Chapter Nine

"Come on and indulge me, Emma. Let's grab this opportunity. I have to go to Jaipur next week to a boring medical conference at one of the big hotels. You remember, Professor Higson and his talks on Malaria? I'm so sorry we won't be able to meet up like we planned."

I was still simmering with anger at Shankar's impromptu appearance. He had taken me completely by surprise by turning up only a week later unannounced on the front steps of Langhousa. What's more, he looked utterly stunning in a white linen suit and starched shirt, which perfectly offset his smouldering sexuality.

I felt a fierce stab of disappointment. "I see, so you're deserting me."

"Come along." He kissed me, light feathery kisses across my face and neck. "Hardly deserting you. You know how these things are?"

"I ought to be angry with you. I told you not to come here," I said.

Shankar leaned against the doorframe. "But, darling, you gave me the impression you wanted to know more about me and to see the other side of me away from the hospital and definitely away from the hotel, so here I am." He glanced past me up the hall. "Besides, there's no one to see me. It's Anya's day off and I was exceedingly careful. I brought the car and hid it down that trail leading to the jungle."

I went to say something, but Shankar was already pushing past me.

"How do you know Anya's not here? You haven't been spying on me, have you?"

He grinned at me. "Good Lord, no. But Anya happens to know the maid at the Apsleys and the two of them go to the market on a Thursday."

"And don't tell me." I pulled a face. "You know the Apsleys?"

"Why, yes of course, my sweet, I know a great many people." He winked at me, pausing for a moment to push me up against a cabinet. "Now, look, I don't want to keep having a sordid affair with you in some little hotel room, and since I adore you, this stage of getting to know one another's inevitable, don't you think?"

There was nowhere to escape to—not that I wanted to anyway. He nudged my legs apart and, rubbing the flimsy silk of my dress between his fingers, slid his one hand up to cup my breast. By now I couldn't hide my reactions. I simply put my hand over his other one and pressed it harder between my legs. He bent to pick up the box lying at his feet by the door. "Actually, I've got a proposition for you." I clung to him hungrily, his gaze drilling into mine. "I want to take you out to see the ruins of Shamir. There's a shrine there."

"Well, you know how to spring a surprise." I led him into the parlour and he sat down beside me on the couch by the window, his warm thigh brushing against mine. After a while, he slipped his arm around my shoulders, drawing me closer, spreading his hand over my belly, then back down between my legs, moving his finger gently back and forth across my wet slit.

Of course I wanted to go to Shamir. Shankar had already told me a lot about the ruins. There were many legends about the old temple that had once been a shrine to the jinn, but unless you knew where it was it was notoriously difficult to find. "Yes, yes, all right." I couldn't hide my enthusiasm. "But I'll have to change into something more suitable. It's jungle, isn't it, there's no road up there?"

"No, only an ancient path. Wear something casual and some good walking shoes."

I dressed in an old pair of Rowena's gardening trousers and a loose shirt and tied my hair back in a scarf, finishing the ensemble off with a pair of scruffy sandals I'd bought in the bazaar. They would do because apparently the walk up to the temple was a rough one and we'd have to park the car down by the river.

It was quiet when we strolled down the road, Shankar carrying the box, the birds singing and the monkeys chattering in the trees. Shankar used the battered Ford for work, and although serviceable, it had seen better days. It coughed and spluttered, necessitating Shankar having to get out several times to look under the hood before climbing back in. Soon we left the main road and started along a narrower potholed and dusty one, leading up to the mountains. Overnight there had been heavy rain and the holes had filled with water, making them treacherous and disguising their depth. Shankar often had to swerve at the last minute to avoid them, sending me lurching against him, clutching his arm and laughing. Eventually the road petered out completely and we were confronted by a virtually impenetrable wall of emerald green jungle. Shankar leaned across the seat. He was hot and a mild sheen of perspiration from the intense humidity beaded his fragrant skin. I kissed him hard on the lips and he looked at me in surprise.

"I've wanted you to be with me like this for ages. My God, you look even more beautiful today." He tucked an errant strand of my hair beneath my headscarf. "Come along, my angel."

I kissed him again, wrapping my arms around his neck. "And what does that make you then, the devil?"

"Well," he quipped. "You already know I consort with devils."

"That's not funny." I pouted.

Opening the car door, he took hold of my hand, running his fingers over it sensually. "Come along."

The air was beginning to hum with that familiar energy I always seemed to feel around Shankar. Taking my arm, he began to lead me up the path, guiding me every so often when I almost stumbled and fell. After a while he pointed through a break in the trees. "This small fork in the road leads to one of the hill villages. It's called Nampir. I frequently take some medicines up there. The people are terribly poor and sick."

"You mean some of the stolen medicines?"

Shankar stopped, raising his eyebrow. "Hell, how do you know about that? I didn't think anyone knew."

"I do. Merkel told me you were in trouble with the hospital—that some of the medicines had gone missing and due to all the work you did with the hill people they suspected you. She also told me something about you having to appear before the review board."

"Oh." He looked at me. "Another black stain on my soul. And how does that make you feel?"

"Look at me." I put my hands on his cheeks. "I love you for you, darling, and I think it's very noble. It shows me what kind of a man you are. You care about other people even to the detriment of yourself. Merkel said you spent every last penny of your aunt's inheritance on medicine for the poor people and then when it ran out you…" Smiling, I smoothed my fingers around his mouth. "Well, you took some medicine you evidently thought wouldn't be missed."

"Yes, that's right, but no one else sees it that way. It was fine in the beginning. I was using the remnants of the inheritance my aunt had left me, but it didn't last long. I only took some out of date medication from the pharmacy nobody would have used. It wasn't like I was robbing the hospital. Now, though, it looks like they're going to strike me off. It seems that whatever I try to do is futile because some dark shadow seems to hover over me, some bad karma. Perhaps you're right, perhaps I am possessed?"

I put my hand on his arm, drawing him to a halt. "Shankar, don't talk like this, it's not like you."

"No, well." He shook his head angrily. "This petty bureaucracy makes me crazy. It was a few old medicines, for heaven's sake. It wasn't like I raided the dispensary." Guiding me through the undergrowth I leaned against him. "It's funny, you know. I wanted to become a doctor, believing that by caring for the sick I could somehow harmonise the dark with the light. Now it seems I'm a petty criminal."

I swallowed past the lump in my throat. "They can't really strike you off, can they?"

"Yes, they can but it doesn't matter since I have a contingency plan. Several years ago when I was still considerably wealthy, a friend of mine died and I bought his old bungalow. It's not far from here. That's part of what I wanted to show you today. It's a good place for a person like me. I think I can live here peacefully. You see, there's still so much you don't know about Shankar Maravar." Walking away backwards from me with his hands raised, he was smiling. "Anyway, let's forget all this worry. Shankar Maravar is a happy man, he's in love."

Chasing him, I punched him playfully in the chest, making him lose his balance and we tangled together, caressing and stroking for a moment. We were standing deep in the jungle and he interlaced our fingers.

"Through there is the path leading to the old bungalow." He pointed. "It's almost in the temple on holy ground and Vasi still lives in the garden. You'll meet Vasi. Come on, let me show you the bungalow first."

We continued up the path and soon I could see a gap in the trees thinning into a clearing and in the middle of this was a ramshackle old bungalow made of peeling white-painted wood and with a rickety veranda. It would once have been exceptionally pretty but now the doors and windows hung open and there were holes in the roof.

"I realise it looks like a bad mess and it needs a lick of paint, but I think with a few repairs it would be nice, don't you?" Shankar was bubbling with enthusiasm.

"That's an understatement, it's falling to pieces." Pushing my way through the undergrowth, I proceeded to walk up the few broken steps.

"Be careful where you put your feet, Emma."

I gazed around, taking in the view down to the valley. All around me I could hear the sound of the jungle — the song of the crickets, the familiar cacophony of birds and monkeys. Before long I was imagining a couple of rattan chairs out on the veranda and maybe a swing where Shankar and I would sit indulging ourselves in our own little world. He was right. Once the undergrowth had been cut back and the bungalow repaired, it could be fabulous.

"Years ago it was a pretty place. I remember having lemonade right where you're standing." He was holding out his arms and now swung me down gently, pressing his muscular body to mine. "Don't you think you could be happy here?"

My heart was thundering. Feeling the ripple of his warm flesh under my hands, I couldn't keep my hands off him and I knew now we were destined to be together. I couldn't imagine myself with any other man.

"*Mem-saab*," a voice called out, startling me so much I lost my footing and Shankar had to grab me.

An old man, the owner of the voice, had appeared on the veranda and he was grinning at us. Vasi looked like an ancient prophet with his long beard down to his waist. He was dressed in an impeccable white dhoti, kurta and turban. What was most surprising about him though was the henna markings on his hands and bare feet and the lovely smile lighting up his face. I was mesmerised and felt a great outpouring of warmth towards Vasi. I liked him immediately — in truth I felt I'd known him my entire life.

"Vasi, you silly man, do you have to creep around so silently?" Shankar grumbled.

"So, this is the *Mem-saab* I've heard so much about?" Turning to me, Vasi studied me carefully, taking my hands in his. "Hello, lovely Miss Emma Spence, you're a very striking woman and I'm very pleased to be meeting you." Then, his attention swivelled to Shankar. "You are right."

"Right about what?" I teased. "What have you been saying about me to your friend Vasi, Shankar?"

"All good things I assure you," Shankar said, pushing his hands in his pockets.

"*Mem-saa*b have aura of great light, very special, very powerful lady," Vasi said in his broken English.

"Don't take any notice of Vasi, he's an old fool. Why did you break your taboo today, Vasi?" Shankar was playfully goading his friend. "You see, Vasi hides like a tiger in this overgrown garden. He's tethered to this mortal world by an even thinner thread than ours, and in order to understand this mortal life, he lives in silent contemplation either here or in the ruins and seldom does he come out of hiding. You're privileged indeed. He must intuit something intriguing about you. Vasi's more than a father and a brother to me, Emma, he's my guide, my inspiration, a man who is far seeing and learned in all things."

"Pah, rubbish," Vasi muttered grumpily, shaking his head and sitting down on the steps to the veranda. "*Mem-saab* Emma, I am thinking you should come to the house of my cousin and she will paint your hands for you. Much protection needed from naughty jinn."

"And why would I need protection from the jinn, Vasi?" I asked.

Vasi grinned at me.

* * * *

"Vasi thinks if he's painted from head to foot in henna he's protected," Shankar explained later on. "He's always lived here like his father and his father before him. They are guardians of this place." Shankar was leading me through a grove of thick banyan trees, the path becoming narrower and more overgrown, the forest floor littered by the squashed fruit the monkeys had been feeding on.

"He liked you and I'm glad. Believe me, if Vasi doesn't like you, you can soon tell. In a way Vasi is like the great Aamir. He spends his life with the jinn, he can see them as clearly as he can see you and I. You'll get to know him better and he'll tell you many things."

"I hope so," I said quietly. "I liked him immensely. But what about the box, Shankar? You already hinted he knew about Bem Hazari and I can't see him agreeing with your friendship with that demon."

Shankar's fingers were interlaced through mine. "You're right, Vasi does know and it's wise not to provoke him, but there's one thing you must understand about Vasi. He sees all of destiny and he does not interfere in its process. It's a hard thing to accept destiny and to watch it and allow it to follow its path, but Vasi believes everything has a higher purpose eventually working out for the betterment of all."

The temple was so well hidden it seemed to blend into the jungle. It was only when Shankar's arm tightened around mine and he drew me to a stop that I actually saw the well-concealed piles of tumbled stones and the ruined walls rising up from the jungle floor.

"Here we are. Do you feel the change in the air? This is such a special place, a forgotten place. A temple where many hundreds of years ago people came to worship the jinn and give offerings to the earth spirits. The small group of holy men who lived here were Vasi's forebears. When the normal priests found out about them, though, they came here and tried to destroy the temple. The jinn priests fled and some of them, like Vasi, have hidden in the jungle ever since."

Carefully stepping over a fallen pile of stones, I found myself within four tumbled-down walls covered in twisted creepers and moss. The temple felt full of strange swirling energies. Holy places and the wildness of nature never failed to stir me because as Rowena had explained to me, I was special and attuned to the elemental energies.

"Can you feel the jinn, they're everywhere, there's even one watching us now."

"Where?" I experienced that familiar creeping feeling up the back of my spine.

"It's up on the wall where the arches meet above your head. Don't look up, it's crawling closer."

I felt a tantalising erotic prickle dart down my spine. Glancing up, I suddenly saw a shadow leap with the agility of a monkey into the trees. It was unlike anything I'd seen before.

"What an ugly little devil he is."

Shankar was gazing at me, stroking my cheek, his expression soft and loving. "I'm so glad I brought you here, Emma. I promised myself I was going to bring the woman I loved to the secret temple. You do realise I love you, don't you?"

"Oh," I joked. "I think I just might by now."

Parting my lips, I let him stroke my mouth and kiss me, a long slow sensuous kiss that stirred me and made me cling to him, hungry and wanting.

"I'm going to ask you something important, Emma. How would you like to be married to a penniless doctor? Perhaps, Miss Emma, the rich heiress, only wants a doctor with a fine house in Delhi or Jaipur? Maybe she couldn't live in a tumbledown bungalow in the middle of the jungle?"

My heart was increasing in tempo. I could hardly believe what I was hearing. "My Lord, Shankar. This isn't what I think it is, is it?"

"A marriage proposal? Well yes, and why not. I've been thinking about this for a long time. You have to agree we're eminently suited in the most important ways." He looked thoughtful, his brow furrowed. "That's not to say it won't be hard. Anglo Indian marriages are never easy. Look at Mrs Fortescue, for instance. She's hardly accepted in polite society, is she? Besides you'd be the wife of a demon hunter and because of that, the butt of the gossips."

"Mrs Fortescue's situation is nothing like ours," I pointed out. "Veer's so much older than Mrs Fortescue, and anyway, I don't care a fig what people think of me. I love you."

And I did, I thought. I loved Shankar Maravar, the demon hunter.

Chapter Ten

The next morning I awoke from a deep sleep to the tattoo of rain drumming on the roof. I'd always found the sounds of the monsoon rain comforting when I was a child but the monsoons had come later this year and they'd taken me by surprise. Tossing and turning, I ran my fingers listlessly through my hair. I'd been very hot and feverish since the walk to the temple and I couldn't stop thinking about what Shankar had said. I sat up, pulled my thin robe around me and wandered to the windows to latch them. It was raining so heavily, the large droplets were falling like darts. I placed my hand on the latch and held out my palm, letting them cascade over my skin. The rain was so renewing I thought, as, winding my hair around my finger, a sudden movement made me glance towards the trees. I could just make out Shankar standing beneath one of the tall banyan trees right by the front gate. I grabbed my umbrella out of the stand in the hall, opened the door, and, braving the rain, I advanced down the path with the umbrella held aloft.

"You're getting soaked. Whatever are you doing here?" I called.

My robe was clinging wetly to my body, outlining every shadowy rise and fall, from my dark thrusting nipples to the darker crescent between my legs. His gaze embraced me, coming to settle on my contours, and I shivered with longing.

"I'm sure you'll admit you're being an idiot standing in the rain. How long have you been here and why didn't you come to the door and knock?"

"Dear Emma." Cupping my chin he drew me close, sliding his hand up my back. "I had every intention. Then I got to the gate and I thought what a fool I'd made of myself yesterday. I should never have got so carried away and said the things I did." I felt his hand edging down farther, fingering my buttocks. "Forgive me, darling."

"What! Forgive you for asking to marry me? I don't think so!" I laughed. The rain was trickling in sensual fingers through my hair and down my neck and even mingling with my own juices between my legs. "Come inside."

Shankar stood in the hall shivering and dripping a large puddle onto the polished floor. "After I dropped you off yesterday, I parked the car and then I came back through the trees. I was going to knock, take you in my arms and make you say, 'Yes, yes, Shankar, I'll be your wife'. Instead, I simply sat and watched you. You were so magical when you came out naked onto the veranda, combing your hair, touching yourself as if you were thinking of me."

"Look, I'll go upstairs and get you something dry to wear. There's still some old stuff of my grandfather's in the spare bedroom."

When I brought the clothes downstairs Shankar had already stripped out of his wet shirt and pants. I still couldn't get over how much his body excited me and I stood for a moment watching him until he saw my reflection in the glass and turned around. I couldn't tear my eyes away from the gentle upward curve of his inviting cock.

I shook out a *dhoti* and helped him into it. Then he sat on the rattan couch by the window, combing his fingers through his wet hair. "I have some bad news, Emma. It's about the hospital. I'm in worse trouble than I thought. The director's suspended me pending investigation. The truth is I lied to you. I'm not going to Jaipur to the medical convention, I'm going to see a friend of mine in the city who's a lawyer and who might be able to help me."

I sat down beside him, my hand on his shoulder. "You're an excellent doctor, surely if you explained to them the reasons why you took the medicine, they'd understand."

"Thank you for your belief in me, darling. However, this is India and I'm an Indian. I'm afraid I won't be given—how do you put it in English—the benefit of the doubt?" He put his hand on my thigh, wriggling it under my robe, finding the warm place that gave me so much pleasure. "I've done a bad thing stealing the medicines and now I must suffer the consequences. By the way, I've left the lodging house where I was staying."

"But if you can't stay at the lodging house where will you stay?" I cried anxiously.

"That's easy, it's really not that bad. I've already taken most of my belongings, including the box, up to the bungalow."

I sat, chewing on my lip and wondering how best to phrase the idea I had in mind. I knew there was nothing for it but just to voice my suggestion. "If you feel you have to, you must go to Jaipur, but leave the box here where you know it's secure. I can look after it. I can put it in the old safe. Then, when you get back, Shankar, you must stay here. It's the monsoon season and the bungalow has no roof. It's impossible for you to live there. You'll die from the cold and wet."

He shook his head slowly, cupping my chin and kissing me. "You know there are so many reasons why I love you, my darling. Thank you."

Any further conversation was cut short as, dropping to his knees and lifting my robe, Shankar began to tease my sex, and with a sigh and stretching my limbs, I abandoned myself to wave after wave of sheer ecstasy.

Chapter Eleven

Shankar did not come back from Jaipur.

At first I wondered if his delay had been caused by the heavy rains that had washed away the bridge and part of the road. But then one day, as I was sitting in an armchair by the window I saw Vasi walking up the path to Langhousa with his head bowed and tears staining his face. I knew what had happened — the realisation sweeping over me, a knifelike pain piercing my heart. Opening the door I collapsed in his arms.

Vasi refused to come in and for ages we sat on the veranda until, taking my hand, he said huskily and in his less than perfect English, "Missy, it is so terrible. Shankar's dead, an accident. An ox cart ran amok in a main street in Jaipur and knocked him down. He was killed in an instant. No suffer at all thank the gods."

"Oh my God, Vasi." I put my head in my hands and began rocking back and forth. "What am I going to do? I can't live without him. I loved him so much." My heart split in two, the pain stabbing and twisting. I could never love another man after Shankar. We had been so deeply connected it was like we both knew what the other was thinking. My hands and feet were cold and I felt my consciousness lifting out of my body. Strangely it was as if both of us had known our passion couldn't last because there had always been a presentiment where our love was concerned. A kind of urgency for us to experience all the love we could in case it was quickly taken away.

Vasi held me tightly, and after a while I laid my head on his lap whilst he stroked my hair. "*Mem-saab*, important to understand Shankar's soul eternal, all soul eternal. His life done here, very good life so taken early by spirit. Now make journey and find everlasting bliss."

"But I don't want him to leave on that journey, he belongs here with me."

Clenching my fist, I felt the anger boiling up. Everlasting bliss, well, where did that leave me? Alone and without the only mortal man who had ever truly connected with me, loved and understood me, that's where. I never wanted to love again.

* * * *

Later on, sitting in front of my mirror brushing my hair, the dark seed of an idea began to germinate and take shape in my mind. It was an inspirational idea, but it was so dark and tainted I even began to wonder if, yes, I was tainted by the Spence women insanity and all those people who whispered about me were right. What was insane about wanting to have Shankar love me and hold me again, though? I stared at my glistening eyes, possessed now by a fevered glow. It seemed outlandish but maybe, just maybe, there was a way to capture my lover's soul and keep him eternally. Granny Rowena had had a book in her old steamer trunk. She'd told me she ought to have burnt it but had continued to keep it from an ardent sense of curiosity. It was a book on dark demon magic, explaining how to capture a soul, trap it and keep it in captivity. A cold shiver, a mixture of both fear and excitement rippled up my spine. What if…?

The opportunity for me to carry out this despicable crime arrived sooner than I thought possible when Vasi knocked on my door and explained to me that because Shankar had had no living relatives he had requested the old man on the event of his death to perform the last purification rites and the releasing of his soul.

My heart gave a little jump. "Vasi, does that mean I can see him one last time?"

"Yes," Vasi said. "That is why I come today, so *Mem-saab* can say goodbye."

Vasi had to support me because I could hardly manage to climb the steps to the bungalow. He'd lovingly washed Shankar's body, draping it with a clean white cloth and had laid it out in the back room that smelt of fragrant herbs and spices.

"You're extremely kind to do this, Vasi."

"Shankar like a son to me, brought many expensive medicines to my daughter's house when she was sick."

I cautiously approached the table where the body was laid out. It was a shock for me to see him lying there, looking so peaceful with his long black hair combed back from his face and his skin so smooth and flawless. I bent forward over the body, stroking my finger across his lips, even in death sensing the shiver of spiritual life. "Oh, Shankar, we'll still be together, I promise you," I whispered, trembling at the thought of the dreadful thing I was about to do.

"Let me stay for the ceremony when you release his soul," I pleaded, proceeding with my clever act and feeling evil as I raised my tear-stained face. "At least let me be alone with him for a few moments so I can say goodbye to his soul. Please, Vasi."

Vasi seemed doubtful. Ever since I'd first met him I'd had the impression he knew exactly what I was thinking and he would, wouldn't he? If what Shankar had said was true and Vasi could see the thread of destiny, he'd know the exact consequences of my wicked actions.

At twilight he took the wrapped body out to the pyre and made an offering of rice and flowers. I watched the ceremony with my hands clasped, feeling strangely numb at the prospect of what I was about to do. It hadn't occurred to me for a moment that the ludicrous project I had in mind might not work. Vasi walked anticlockwise around the pyre touching the crackling Kush grass to its base. At that stage I wanted to leap forward screaming, 'No, no.' Instead, I watched the thin curling smoke and the leaping flames and I'm sure within the heart of them I could see the face of Shankar smiling at me and saying, 'Yes, Emma, this thing you do, it's the right thing.'

I sat for ages with my eyes screwed tightly shut, holding the long sleeve of my dress over my mouth to prevent the worst of the stench of burning human flesh. I knew that for what came next I'd have to be brave, very brave indeed. Vasi looked serious raising his bamboo stick, getting ready to bring it crashing down on the fragile skull of my beloved to release his soul.

Afterwards I was left alone and there was no sound except the birds returning to the trees and the occasional crackle of hot ash from the fire.

There was no time to be nervous. I knew I had to be quick to avoid Vasi seeing me. I rushed across to the bushes growing in profusion at the side of the bungalow, and, pulling out the box, I slid the book and keys Shankar had given me for safe keeping, from beneath my dress before darting back to the pyre with its grisly remains.

Opening the lid of the box I began reciting the words from the book and yes, a light like a firefly began glowing inside the cavity of the skull. I held my breath in wonderment for what was being played out was so fantastical I couldn't believe my eyes. Shankar's soul was there exactly like I knew it would be and all I had to do was use all the force of my will to persuade the flickering light to creep forth from its bony home and take up residence in the compartment of black mysteries.

The soul took some enticing, the bright frosted orb hovering in front of me, so close I couldn't resist the temptation of cupping my hands around it and feeling my beloved's deepest most intimate life force. Thank goodness for my occult gifts and knowledge of that other world, for I was sure a lesser woman would have fainted from the beauty of such a whimsical and ephemeral thing. The world swung vertiginously and I had to take some deep breaths to restore myself while tantalising sensations crept up my arms and my mind filled for a moment with a feeling of such euphoria I thought I must have been dreaming. The light then moved slowly into the box and, closing the lid, I hid it once more in the tangle of bushes.

Chapter Twelve

I would soon be guilty of more than one heinous crime and I felt like everyone was watching me and knew what I was about to do. Anya looked suspicious, Vasi stayed away from me and my old monkey friend wouldn't come and sit in my lap, but watched me, his brow furrowed, doubtless intrigued by the feral energies clinging to me. The monkey had once loved leaping indoors and snatching pieces of fruit out of my fingers. Since I'd done the second terrible thing and captured Shankar's soul, though, he kept his distance and if I moved suddenly his body tensed and his teeth barred in a snarl. Sometimes he even clambered up into the trees where he sat chattering at me and throwing pieces of fruit and no wonder. Animals are so perceptive and I was tainted – tainted with demon and black magic. I shivered, drawing my thin robe about me.

The Aeolian harp spun above my head in the breeze and I tightened my fists on the arms of my chair. I'd known one day I'd go to Mr Bodekar on the fateful day Marion had mentioned him. Mr Bodekar came from deepest Africa where he had learnt a powerful kind of black magic enabling him to conjure bodies back to life and form hideous creatures out of smoke and ethers. He was supposedly one of the most feared conjurors of black magic in India, not that that put me off—no, not at all. I wanted a dark conjuror and the darker the better. If the price was right, there was nothing Mr Bodekar wouldn't do.

Ever since I'd held Shankar's soul in my hand I'd known the path destiny would take and I was not ashamed to admit I was once again craving the feel of a pair of warm hands, fruity, thrusting kisses and a hot cock inside me. But a soul was a soul and it was like Shankar's old Ford without the engine—it was doing nothing and going nowhere without some form of animation, namely a body to house it and the semblance of warm flesh and blood. The way I saw it, I had no option. I was only human, desperately alone and out of my mind with sobbing hysteria over my lover. Mr Bodekar could give me what I wanted.

The night before I left for Delhi with my precious cargo I slept surprisingly well with the box beside me on the bed. I hadn't gone into details, but I'd recently mentioned to Merkel about my plan and Merkel had been horrified. "My Lord, Emma, don't stoop so low, don't dabble in the black arts, you don't know how dangerous it is."

"What's so terrible about wanting my lover back?" I'd retorted.

Chapter Thirteen

When I got up on the morning of the fateful crime I was in high spirits. Sitting on the veranda I watched Anya pour my tea, her black button eyes sorrowful and accusatory.

"Make sure Stockley's ready on time, won't you? I don't want to be late." I smiled.

Anya put down the teapot with a terrific rattle. She was frowning. "*Mem-saab* Emma?"

"Yes, Anya."

She was wringing her hands and she seemed awfully nervous. "This thing you do, this going to see the bad man Mr Bodekar, it makes all the spirits very angry. I put many cakes down by the pool, but jinn still being naughty and steal washing and pickles off back step. Please, this be making bad luck. When you play with and open box, milk turn and monkey not come for fruit, and plant with big flowers begin to die."

Astonished at this outburst, I stared at her critically. "Anya, most of this is your imagination. You know you shouldn't have listened in to my conversation when Miss Merkel was here, you were bad to do that."

I sipped my tea while Anya stood wringing her hands. "Yes, *Mem-saab*, I know, but bad thing *Mem-saab* do, going to talk to demon man."

"No, Anya." I tugged my robe around my shoulders. "Mr Bodekar will make me happy and I'll be much more like the old Emma and you'd like for everything to be back to normal and for me not to be quite so sad and bad-tempered, wouldn't you?"

"If *Mem-saab* says so." Anya shrugged. She was full of superstition having been brought up in a household fearing evil spirits and she greedily looked for evidence of conniving jinn spirits everywhere. She could read fate in two crossed sticks on the veranda or the musical thump of a banging door. She was continually reciting the Vedas in the constant belief that so much holy repetition prevented her succumbing to the predatory behaviour of the jinn and protected her from black magic. Most of all she was positively petrified of men like Mr Bodekar – but then again Mr Bodekar was a legend. It seemed everyone knew and feared him, even David, who had mentioned he'd once seen Mr Bodekar crossing the road at the Delhi market dressed in black robes and looking like the devil himself.

I went upstairs and put on a plain black gown and lace gloves. Pinning up my hair, I next glanced at myself in the mirror. I was exceedingly pale. "You do know this is a bad thing you do, Emma Spence," I murmured. Why then did I feel so ebullient and suffused by an anticipatory warm glow? I came downstairs and stood for a moment staring at the box sitting on the table, before shaking out the black silk used to cover it. I then wrapped it up in the hessian sacking and put it under my arm.

Stockley was just coming cautiously around the sweeping gravel drive in the car he despised. Stockley was very old now and so bent double he could hardly see over the steering wheel. Despite having been my family's chauffeur for so long, the car was still as much a demon to him as Mr Bodekar was to Anya, and every inch of the way to our destination would be fraught with the grating of gears and a huge amount of swearing. I smoothed my gloves, then slid onto the backseat and slammed the door.

I felt like crying when I thought of what I was about to do and I clung to the box like a sailor thrown overboard might cling to his lifebelt. I knew there was still time to change my mind, but how could I? Shankar, a mortal man, had been able to open my heart and mind and show me what bliss could be, and now he'd been mercilessly snatched away. There was only one way to get him back and that was by using less than orthodox means. But still I felt bad about it and I felt even worse now that I'd placed the soul in the box with that legendary reprobate – such an act being tantamount to madness. My only consolation was that by Shankar's own admission the box was truly a spiritual stronghold and the perfect place for the safe keeping of his soul, and furthermore, he'd had a fascination with Bem. I stroked the box lovingly. Why, it was like the legend of Pandora's Box, except Shankar's sinful box of treasure contained one inspiring message of hope for everlasting love – my lover's soul.

It was extremely humid and I wound the window down a fraction. Lately I was always feeling warm.

Perhaps it was the thought of the demon magic of the jinn, those elementals born of fire.

I gazed about myself.

How beautiful everything seemed today. I caressed and stroked the wood, even contemplated whispering to it, while the sinful repository of arcane temptations bumped against my leg. We continued to drive along the winding road through the lowlands, between lush green jungle, and in the distance a glimpse of the mountains tipped with their veils of low cloud.

It was quite a drive to Delhi and soon we came upon men beating cattle with sticks and women with strange bundles balanced on their heads. Stockley took no notice of all of this. Instead he wove precariously from side to side, honking his horn and making me hang onto my seat.

It was a tiring, dusty journey but eventually we were battling our way into the city. Unfolding the small piece of paper in my purse, I looked at the directions.

Stockley pulled over, got out of the car and opened the door for me.

"Thank you, Stockley."

"Miss Emma, are you all right to walk all the way on your own?"

"Perfectly all right, thank you." I frowned, glancing up and noticing a woman draw back into a doorway. She seemed to be watching me. "Go on to the hotel and wait for me like we arranged."

Stockley had taken off his cap and was slapping it on his thigh. "I don't know if I like leaving you here, miss."

"Stockley. I'll be fine," I replied, wrestling the swaddled box off the back seat. I was sure I could hear Shankar's trapped soul castigating me from his wooden prison.

I tried to balance the box as I sidestepped overflowing gutters and dogs who followed me with haunted expressions. I asked several people if they'd heard of Mr Bodekar since I didn't seem able to find the street, but his name seemed to strike fear into everyone and they gazed at me sullen and tight-lipped. Crossing the market square, I hesitated before another of the seemingly identical alleyways. "Please could you tell me where I might find Mr Bodekar?" I asked a woman. Her dark, kohl-rimmed eyes peered at me through diaphanous material. With a shiver I realised this was actually the woman I had noticed before.

"Do not be scared, please to come with me. Mr Bodekar said English girl not know how to find way."

"So, you're the messenger from Mr Bodekar? He said he might send someone to watch out for me."

"Yes, miss. I had to be sure it was you. No one know exact place of Mr Bodekar," she muttered.

I followed her up the narrow alleyway, between a shambolic confusion of tumbledown houses with curtains across doorways and confusing little side streets. Until, almost losing her, my guide darted up a narrow passage no wider than a person's body. We edged our way down this corridor until we came to the door of a large building, whereupon the woman took a key out from under her sari and, turning it in the lock, ushered me inside. I was now in a cool villa with a mosaic floor and high ceilings around which ran a balcony. I could hear the distant echo of voices, smell cooking food and hear some kind of music. It was baffling. Catching hold of my arm, she drew me into a doorway and I blinked. It was gloomy and I felt like I'd stepped over an evil threshold into an entirely grimworld, but surely love would forgive all.

Mr Bodekar was sitting in an armchair near a huge carved table. He was not what I'd anticipated. I'd expected a wizened old man. Instead, despite his forbidding aura, he was darkly appealing with eyes which seemed to reach inside me and read my thoughts. I stood for a moment, trembling and inhaling the powerful incense whilst the candles flickered. Mr Bodekar, dressed in loose flowing black robes and with long black hair down to his waist, peered at me intently, his gaze flicking from time to time to the box under my arm.

"Eyes of soul," he said suddenly. "Very pretty woman, Miss Spence." Curiously in that instant, his eyes seemed to become blacker and for some reason I gripped the box tighter. I was terribly scared but I kept telling myself that if nothing else Mr Bodekar was trustworthy. Apparently he had even woven magic for Indian royalty.

"So white woman come to Bodekar? You understand my reputation, miss? I weave what most people term bad magic." He grinned at me. "It must be strong spell you want, to be brave enough to come to Bodekar."

Wetting my lips I stood my ground, my legs trembling. "I won't waste your precious time," I said bravely, my mouth as dry as ashes. "I need you to conjure me a commodious human body to house a soul. You see, Mr Bodekar, I was to marry a man and he died and now his soul is in this box for safekeeping. He was a jinn master." Taking a deep breath, I attempted to gather my frayed nerves. I knew what I was next going to say would sound crazy to anyone else. "Mr Bodekar, I've discovered I'm a selfish woman because I want my lover back. I've trapped his soul and I want you to put that soul back in a body." Placing the box for a moment on a chair, I took the photograph of Shankar from out of my purse where I carried it and I placed it in front of him. "I'm open-minded, I know such things are possible and I know since you're the most powerful conjuror in India, you can perform this act of magic."

Mr Bodekar turned the picture around, then he began stroking his chin. "Mmm, I see. I think this will be requiring a great many rupees." His glance shifted to the box, his lips narrowing into a thin line. "Unwrap box, please."

My throat felt so tight now, I could hardly swallow. "Yes, Mr Bodekar." I took off the hessian and, unwrapping the black silk, placed the box on the table.

"All such boxes have keys and books. Please to also be letting me see them," he said in his fractured English.

Reluctantly, I took the chain from around my neck, then taking the book out of my coat pocket, I put it on the table.

Mr Bodekar's expression was inscrutable. "Ah, my goodness, a jinn box made by the legendary Ravrankar. These boxes are worth a fortune and Miss should not be carrying it around to be visible to every thief. Of course, in other circumstances I might offer to buy it from you, but I do not deal in artefacts anymore and besides, I already have the most powerful box in the world, in my care." He leant forward, pressing his ear to the wood. "These boxes can be very seductive. Why, I can hear it has a noisy beast inside it and this jinni has terribly loud voice. Have you peeped inside and has its occupant spoken to you?" Mr Bodekar tapped the box with the key. "It isn't your lover. This is a devil, a powerful ancient spirit, Miss Spence, and it has seduced the soul of your beloved who, it seems, did not put up much of a fight. Your lover has a thirst for darkness and conceded easily." He leant back folding his hands. "Please sit down, Miss Spence. I can tell you find what I say disturbing, but you know it's true, don't you?"

I sat down heavily in the chair opposite Bodekar. I was either talking to a genius or I was more of a fool than I thought. Peering in my purse, I took out a wad of money and handed it over. "This is the agreed sum you stated in your message. You can count it if you like. Now, Mr Bodekar, I didn't come here to talk about the box."

"No, Miss Spence, but this mysterious box plays an important part in this mystery, wouldn't you agree?" He continued to rhythmically stroke his chin. "I must warn you, I know of this jinni spirit and his ancient name is Bem Hazari, a shaitan and king of the elementals. He's a creature who thirsts for sex of all permutations, since his diet of sex and human sex energy is what makes his powers grow and leads him towards his goal of ecstatic sexual transformation. A process, I might add, which takes many centuries. Such a thirst makes him dangerous and like a man in the desert who has been without water for many days, he will do anything to assuage that thirst."

"Yes, I know." I gasped, struggling to loosen the top button of my blouse. I suddenly felt faint.

Bodekar fixed me with his piercing gaze. "Miss Spence, I like you. You're a brave woman and you must have power to conjure a soul into the box. However, most of the conjuration was due to the demon Bem Hazari who enticed the soul and used you without your knowledge as the instrument. You're fascinating but I'm afraid you have only weak powers in commanding souls." He steepled his fingers. "There's still time to go home and forget this idea, Miss Spence, although I know all about the pain of love and the human spirit and how it can drive us to do the maddest things. I'm a jinn demon just like Bem Hazari and like Bem I enjoy being amongst humans and there is much good about being human. If I make you a body, though, you must understand that although it will seem real, it will not be and can never be your lover, though it might look and smell like him. It will be the coat for Bem Hazari and merely the house for Shankar's soul and even though I say so myself" — he chuckled evilly — "a fine coat it will be."

"Mr Bodekar, I've made my decision. Fashion me this body," I said, breathing shallowly, my heart palpating. "Please do it and let's have done with it."

"Mmm." Bodekar stealthily rose to his feet and spent a moment or two pacing the room like a wraith, his overpowering charismatic energies descending over me in a cloud. Eventually he seemed to come to a decision, and after sitting back down and arranging his robes around him, he fingered the wad of bills. "Miss Spence, there are grave dangers. These boxes are prisons and there's a good reason why these spirits are kept captive. If I make you the illusory human coat you will release the demon Bem Hazari into the outside world. He has been many centuries in his dark prison and at the moment he is much weaker than he was. But once he gets the liberty he craves, he'll be driven to feed and the more he feeds, the stronger he'll grow until there's no telling what he might be capable of."

"So I've heard," I replied, gripping the arms of the chair savagely, a fizzing sensation starting at the base of my spine. The thought of seeing Shankar's face was too much for me to bear.

"Fine, I can see you're decided, Miss Spence. I make excellent spirit coat, warm like human body. Miss leave box with me, then tomorrow return at midday."

Chapter Fourteen

Shankar stepped out of the shadows, moving with the sinuous stealth of a panther and not a man. He was completely naked, brutally provocative, and being born now from spirit and no longer flesh and blood, more desirable than he ever had been when a mortal. I couldn't tear my gaze away from the sight of his gently curving spine flowing into those perfectly uplifted buttocks and the covering of smooth burnished copper skin.

I cried out, my breath catching, the book I'd been reading earlier falling open onto the floor. Woken up from a dream of tender caresses, I was still woven within the fabric of the astral planes, having fallen asleep exhausted from my sobbing.

"Hush," he said tenderly, sitting down on the couch, teasing my stockings and next unclipping one of them and rolling it down my leg.

I blinked rapidly, not sure for a moment if I was still asleep, but I knew this touch and it was very familiar. After all, I'd been reliving it in my mind ever since Shankar's death. Now, when I opened my eyes a crack, I saw Shankar peering at me and he had changed, I could see that. His rebirth from the realm of dark spirit had embellished him with such spiritual finery, the air hummed and a nimbus of what could only be termed fire crackled around him.

"You always liked to wake up with my finger in your cunt." He grinned, leaning forward mischievously.

"Shankar I..." My words trailed off as he placed his finger across my lips.

His voice was different—it was hard to say in what way, but it seemed deeper, more alluring. The room was dark, lit by a dull glow from the last remaining guttering spell candle on the table, and it was then I saw the open box and I recalled how earlier I'd opened it, lit the candles and sat chanting the spell Mr Bodekar had given me. The incantations had been fruitless at first and nothing had happened. Night after night I did what I'd been told to do, marshalling my mental strength, willing the dark spectre to appear. Mr Bodekar hadn't disbelieved for a moment that his magic would work. But maybe despite my belief in otherworld forces this was the mortal world and my subconscious human mind kept niggling away at me, making me doubt the manifestation of the spectre and preventing the spell from completing. Driven by love and desire, I had chanted fervently. Every night I had burnt the herbs Mr Bodekar had given me, making sure the moon had been at its most propitious when I had lit the black candles and had drawn the symbols of conjuration the magician had shown me and now...my heart was beating so fast the room seemed to be spinning. Now, here he was.

"How peculiar." He smoothed his hand up his arm. "Mr Bodekar is a skilled magician because this body feels even better than the human one. It fits me like a glove and if anything is a thousand times more sensitive." His eyes gleamed, his delicious lips curving upwards, mouth slightly open in devilish invitation.

"And what's this?" He stood up and wandered over to the candle on the table, staring at it, mesmerised by its guttering light. "Oh fire, how I love it, Emma. Yes, I'm born of fire."

I gasped, putting my hand over my mouth in horror when he passed his hand across the naked flame and a greedy, near madness—occasioned by the flickering orange light—leapt in his eyes. I wasn't dreaming and the realisation of this sent charges prickling across the surface of my skin. Bem—I knew that's who now had dominion over my lover's body—turned from his appraisal of the candle and my heart beat even faster. Experimental etheric fingers—the stuff of ghostly tales—extended from his hands in cords of light and teased aside my clothes, rippling up my thighs and becoming more insistent. Wriggling back on the couch I tried to clamp my legs together. I'd never seen anything like it and whilst I was fascinated, I was also scared by this spirit invasion.

"Emma, Emma." Smiling, he advanced on me, his cock firm and gently uplifted, the tip glistening invitingly. "Don't be alarmed, darling. You can see I'm the same but exquisitely embellished. I am now a creature of many senses and I have many methods to tantalise you with and many lovely ways of arousing you. You'll see, it'll be even more wonderful than before." Sinking down beside me, he began raising the hem of my dress, trickling his finger over my skin, whilst entranced, I held my breath.

"Look at me, darling. You'll see it's me."

I didn't have to, because I could feel him in the subtle energies now swirling around me. I could sense Shankar's soul beneath his tantalising demon overcoat and in his eyes I could also see the flicker of an occult flame leaping in response to my lust. My body was humming in orgasmic delight and my skin erupted in response to the million enticing fingers creeping over my skin. I tightened my fists and my mouth opened in an 'O' of pleasure.

"Yes, Emma. The temptation of sex and love and Mr Bodekar's ingenuity have given birth to me. Isn't it a wondrous thing?"

I fingered the keys around my neck, feeling them reassuringly anchored there by my gold chain. "If I was to bid you go back in the box, would you obey me?" I asked shakily.

"What's this, you only just bring me here and immediately you talk of being my mistress, of controlling me and sending me back?" The smile died on his lips. "I'm your Lord Bem, your genie in a bottle but, yes mistress, it's true. I'm at your command." He crawled stealthily forwards, looking more like a creature than a man. "You see I'm changed and yet I'm still the same."

My goodness. I bit my fist. It was unbelievable. Yes, here was my darling Shankar. I glanced around I was sure that the room was full of invisible stuff more refined than the real world, glittering spots of light like the bright drifting ashes from the pyre.

"I can tell you this world of fabulous sensations takes some getting used to, for now I'm no longer an entity of airy and fiery substance," he explained. "Now thank the gods I have the semblance of a flesh and blood vehicle imbued with the immortality of Bodekar's creation."

I touched his arm, smoothed my fingers up and down. There was a dark burning luminosity in Bem's eyes and his body was pulsing and trembling under my touch.

"You're so gorgeous, Emma. Come to me and don't be afraid."

I wriggled up the couch away from him, my heart thumping as he trapped me, teasing open the buttons on my dress, circling my nipples, pressing his lips to my skin. "Kiss me," he crooned. "Emma, why won't you kiss me? Do I have to enchain you?"

I tried to push him away, but I could feel tantalising etheric tendrils curling tightly around me in an exquisite symphony, until I found it difficult to move my arms and legs. All the elements and powers, it seemed, were at his command. He kissed me hard on the lips, bruising my tender flesh, and I drew away shocked, putting my hand to my lips. His touch seared like a hot knife, but for all that it wasn't unpleasant and I enjoyed it and felt compelled to kiss him back.

"The wondrous machinations of karma and magic have created this miraculous state of affairs and contrived to bring us together. Now, you can have your fantasy, Emma, because a mortal man was never enough for you, was he?"

I leapt to my feet, wrestling and tugging with the invisible threads. "No," I cried, backing away. "I don't know who you are anymore." Stumbling across the passage I ran into the bedroom, then after turning the key, leant back against the door, my heart hammering. Sliding down onto the floor with my head in my hands, I began to sob.

"Emma, it's me," a voice said after a moment, but this time it sounded ancient and even more mellow and inviting. "I love you and I intend to possess you and show you the delights of my kingdom. Don't be afraid of me."

"I'm not afraid of you," I retorted shakily and I wasn't. No, the more I thought about it the more I realised I was more afraid of myself and the yearnings of my still mortal body. I bit my fist and rubbed at my invisible clinging bonds. I wanted to scream. Is this how it felt to be going insane?

"Emma. Open the door and let me in."

I sat hugging my knees. I was confused because the compulsive draw I felt towards Bem was even stronger than the one I'd had for Shankar, and what's more I was sure I could feel Bem pushing at the closed doors of my mind, filling it with writhing, lurid images. How could I feel such burgeoning passion for a being as dark as Bem? "No, go away, I command you." I groaned, turning and clutching the keys around my neck.

After a while I felt a draught creeping beneath the door, and looking down, I gave a barely perceptible whimper of alarm. The draught had taken the form of thin wisps of smoke. Leaping to my feet and stumbling backwards, I tripped onto the bed, my dress tangling around my legs, my mouth open in surprise. The tendrils of smoke were materialising into Bem, first his hands and arms, next his torso. He was smiling at me, holding his hands out. There was nothing for it. I'd have to make a dash for the door. I darted forward, but Bem was too fast and too strong for me in my state of etheric bondage and, making a grab for me, I only just managed to evade him. It seemed there was no escape, because once again he was moving sinuously forwards, his burnished skin gleaming in the moonlight and I felt those silken skeins drawing tighter and tighter against my flesh. Clawing at the sheets, my heart hammering, I surrendered and he pinned me down and began caressing my skin. I was melting shamelessly, the biting threads spurring me to further lust.

"My, my, what a naughty girl, capturing my soul and having that heathen Mr Bodekar conjure this dark body. But I forgive you, Emma, because you've given me the thing I most wanted." He kissed my cheeks, eyes and lips. "A fabulous vehicle in which to masquerade and indulge in the pleasures of a woman's flesh." Pausing, he grinned at me. "And you don't have to feel bad for Shankar's soul since he embraced me willingly. He's always had a fascination with my kind." Bem eased the dress from my body until I was writhing naked under him. Somehow the silken skeins were pulling my limbs up towards the bedposts so I was spread out. The strange thing was I liked this bondage, this sexual teasing.

"I'd never hurt you, Emma, I'm a creature of hedonism. Of course a little resistance is fun." He ran his tongue over his lips. "I can burn you with my desire, Emma." Winding a strand of my hair around his finger, he tugged it, making me vibrate with a pain that soon settled into a throbbing pulse in my womb.

Second by second I was drawn down farther into his dark seductive world and my resolve weakened. Our faces only a fraction apart, I opened my lips in invitation. Oh yes, why not? I'd missed him so much and now I was being tugged deeper towards his sinister pool of longing. Shimmering electrical charges rippled across the surface of my skin, leaving small circles of burning delight. I jerked on the restraints but miraculously I somehow seemed to be firmly fastened by these invisible bonds of etheric matter. Bem seemed to sense exactly what I was thinking because then followed the most wondrous experience of my life as for the first time I was truly the prisoner of a man or, should I say, a demon. He drew me to such heights of lust I was soon begging him to release me so I could touch and hold him. The torment went on for ages whilst he tested the boundaries of my slowly developing masochistic hunger and stretched me wide open, his glistening penis over my hole, the nub teasing me as he advanced and withdrew it an inch or so. I dug my nails into his soft demon flesh and he shivered with the bliss of it, his cock lifting and tightening even more.

"Pale mortal love is simply a shadow of what I can give you, Emma." Kissing and devouring me, he pulled me roughly into his arms, and with a sigh I lay against him, my body aching for completion. "You know how you told me you knew there was more to a simple human fuck, well, it's true. Humans retain remnants of the memory of spirit love given to them at the birth of the world when human were spiritual beings. When that vital connection was lost humans forgot what true union was. Special people like you, though, Emma, you retain the memory and you share in it with me." His eyes were glistening with emotion. Bem had once again slithered between my legs and was searching for my core. "You see, I can give you the love you truly want, since I have every atom of Shankar's memory but I am also Bem, Lord of the Elementals, Lord of Sex. Ah..." He sighed and thrust his tongue deeply into my mouth. "You're enough to tempt the devil, you exquisite creature. The smell of you, the taste of you."

I screamed and thrashed in passion, erupting in warm convulsions when he grasped my entire mound in his hand, inserting not just one but three fingers up to the hilt deep inside me and thrusting into my slippery flesh, straddling me and driving me deeper against the sheets. "You beast." My moans rose, my head rolled back in a gesture of helpless ecstasy "But, I love you. Do anything." It was like another force had control of me now. I lay splayed and open and at the mercy of his demonic, mesmerising stare.

His hand closed tightly on my breast, squeezing. "Let me kiss you like you dream of being kissed." He rolled his thumb and forefinger over my rigid nubs.

"Mmm, wonderful. Yes, touch me, hold me."

I whimpered, surrendering to the blissful feel of his teeth teasing my skin, travelling down my neck to seize my nipples and roll them around in his mouth. He continued to tease and play between my legs, easing aside the tender fleshy lips to stroke, to circle my hard pleasure bud, my entire body aching for him. Countless times he brought me to the apex of aching orgasmic joy with those lips and fingers.

* * * *

I must have fallen asleep, because I awoke to the roll of thunder and the feel of his fingers still playing inside me. Would it never end? He smiled at me, his thick dark hair falling across his face. "I have something for you," he murmured. "Whilst you were sleeping I brought it for you from my world." He was holding up an exquisite anklet fashioned of Indian silver, inlaid with precious gems, turquoise, tourmaline and ruby, and in-between each gem was a bell.

"Ooh, it's lovely." I was incredulous. How could something like this come from his world? By now, though, I was willing to accept that if Mr Bodekar could make a mortal overcoat for Bem, anything was possible.

"Let me put it on for you." He fastened the anklet around my ankle. "Now, even in that dark place I can hear you."

All demon jinn, find bliss in all things. They enjoy the sound of bells and music, the wind in the trees and the drum of raindrops summoning them and sending them into a trancelike state of ecstasy. Bem was no exception.

His thumb moved in circles over my fiery skin. I was insatiable and aching for more of his touch. "Yes, oh yes." I was moving in a warm sea, the rhythm of the waves washing me gently to and fro.

Shankar had been a stimulating and thoughtful lover, but there was something about Bem, dirty and alluring like he wanted to discover me inside and out. He pinned my wrists to the bed, subjecting me once more to his demon licking and sucking. Spirit matter feeling like fingers, passed through flesh, tugging on my energy points, teasing me to heights of sensation I'd only dreamt about. I kissed him back ardently, any fear forgotten as our tongues tangled and he seduced me all over again. His turgid organ was balanced against my fleshy entrance and I gripped it, manoeuvring it inside me. He laughed wickedly, his finger thrusting high up inside me, finding my sacred seed, while I jerked and shuddered in convulsions of joy.

I grasped the demon's girth, jerking him inwards, unable to control my craving and wanting the sinuous thing even deeper.

"Give it to me," I cried, spreading my legs impossibly wide, as his cock nosed aside my fragile skin and began massaging my delicate walls. Like Marion I'd become a burning, writhing torch of lust and all I wanted to do was feed my desire, propel my own lust higher. Mortal love had never been like this. No wonder Marion had been so obsessed with her demon lover. She'd been right — demon love had fingers that could scintillate every inch of mortal woman's body, in tireless, sexual syncopation.

Of course, I knew that Bem had seduced many human women before, had crept in his ghastly jinn form through many an open window and looked down upon mortal woman's spread limbs. Well, I was determined he would never have a love like mine.

Bem was insatiable as he explored me within the fleshy capsule Bodekar had made for him, indulging himself in every debased act he could think of. No wonder women were driven insane by these dark demonic temptations, these demon seducers — throwing themselves off cliffs, tearing out their hair and nails and retiring into insanity. Turning my head, I glanced at myself in my wardrobe mirror and I saw a woman I didn't recognise, a woman surfing close to that womanly and triumphant union, the explosion at the core of her inner star. My mouth an open pink maw ready to plunder, my fingernails driving deeply into flesh. My face was ghostly white and yet opalescently beautiful.

He rested inside me, caressing my hard ecstasy bud that had earlier given me so much joy, his slick shaft momentarily laying inert, beginning to twitch once more. Again and again he drew me back from the brink of satisfaction, before plunging back in and starting the driving need all over again. He intuited my womanly rhythms and from my scent and heat he knew exactly when to stop and start the momentum to give me the most pleasure. The back and forth pistoning of his fleshy pole plunged me into deeper, more occult enjoyment than I could ever have imagined and instantly, I was rising beyond my human self, every atom of me clenching and unclenching. I was now in a place of wild turbulent energies and fermenting passion and the orgasm burned me, little fires in the palms of my hands and the soles of my feet. He came and put his mouth in these places, quenching the fires and starting a deeper fire in my core. I pushed my breasts up for his greedy mouth and he chewed my nipples, causing hot flashes of sweet pain. Next, gliding down he seized my clit between his teeth and gave me what I wanted. He shook it from side to side and licked the sensitive tip, sending me into paroxysms of ecstasy.

"What are you doing to me?" I groaned through clenched teeth, my mind in free fall while the erotic torture continued. Demon love once tasted was truly obsessive.

"Emma," he whispered, rolling me onto my side. "I love you, darling Emma." Coming into me from behind, he grasped my sex, titillating me with finger and thumb, his entire, dripping length sliding inside my fluid tunnel, feathering that tender, sensitive place until I couldn't control myself. Another orgasm tore through me and I became like a burning, bursting bud, erupting and convulsing in one delightful shock wave after another into a place of exploding suns.

Chapter Fifteen

Part Three

The Present

I'd been living with my elemental lover for three months, and day by day the mortal world was becoming finer and less substantial—the fiery, roiling passion stronger.

Waking up, I opened my eyes and a watery moon spun a skein across the floor. In sleep my mind had retreated to that other place and I floated on drifting velvet clouds, tossed here and there between worlds. If I happened to wake suddenly as I did right then, it was like the thin veil between this world and the other was permeable and I existed in two worlds at the same time, then it took me a moment to gather the strings of mortal and hold fast. The doors were open and the earlier monsoon rains had dried, but on the veranda one pool was left gilded in moonlight and within it the jinn spirits jumped and danced like fireflies. I laid spellbound, captivated by the acuity of my new ultra-sensual world. Even the surface of my skin had become an agonising tool of arousal. I slithered silently off the bed and, pushing open the door, stood naked on the veranda, letting the breeze play on my skin and waiting to see if it would become another orgasmic ecstasy as I experienced a series of fabulous aftershocks. I'd discovered I could have wilful orgasms now from almost anything — the touch of raindrops and the breeze, my clothing — so scratchy and alien, and the thought of Bem whilst warm-scented rose bathwater lapped inside me. I ran my hands up my thighs. What a sensual, epicurean woman I was.

I'd always loved the feel of satin and silk, but now my fine underwear stayed in my drawer unused since I preferred my own sensitised mortal skin, that I powdered and perfumed in readiness for the Bem's next invasion. A curious alchemy was taking me over and my carnal appetites were running out of control. I was changing in fascinating ways during a process whereby my cells and the very structure of my humanity crumbled away and became infused by fantastical desire. What was smooth seemed smoother still. I was damp with continual sex and sometimes hot and clammy with fever. Bem made me dip my toe in sordid delights with the merest suggestion, and things I'd never before contemplated filled me with such excitement my entire body raged.

A beetle spread its black wings and landed at my feet and I could hear the click of its feet magnified a thousand times. How strange, but tonight I was sure I was not at all human anymore. Every creature, leaf and flower seemed to be surrounded by a halo of light. A breeze made the thin curtains blow inwards and a trapped mosquito buzzed loudly. Subconsciously, I reached for the key around my neck, and for an instant a stirring of terror communicated itself to me. I really ought to lock the box more often because I allowed Bem far too much liberty.

I glanced out over the garden, mesmerised by the large raindrops that were beginning to fall again. Each one glistened and vibrated with a life of its own and I could see it alive with the creative element of the jinn. *I'm trapped,* I thought, letting the breeze whisper against my skin. It was not the same kind of entrapment as a marriage or a loveless affair. I was trapped with lust by the demon Bem. At the thought of him my body began to melt and I could imagine him kneeling between my legs, licking the juices trickling down the inside of my thighs while I spread my legs and peeled back my lips for the passage of his inquisitive tongue. I fantasised over pushing his face into my cunt and he obliged, lapping at it like an animal, saying he couldn't get enough of my sweet nectar. Next, he tortured me, sucking the nectar out from inside me. Using his tongue to tickle my velvet walls before I greedily licked the sperm from his stem. With his refined senses he revelled in every odour and globule and the flavours of my human skin, telling me I was like the most delicious fruit, and even when I wasn't that ripe he knew if he kept licking me I'd soon become rich and fragrant. He explained how the droplets on my legs tasted differently to the moisture on my sex lips, and the juices around my sacred spot were different to my ejaculate. My cheeks flared for a moment at the memory of such sticky, sordid torments. In its turn, his sex seed now fed me and sustained me and I couldn't imagine living without it. At first I'd been afraid of tasting demon issue and I'd tried to resist feeding from that juicy stem. However, the stuff was addictive and the simple delight of licking and caressing his tight, sinuous tool and swallowing it down deep into me—the smooth muscles of my throat coaxing a cry from this wicked denizen—filled me with immeasurable satisfaction. My fingers trickled over my still sex-slick skin and I blushed remembering our dirty games. Bem enjoyed bathing me in his sticky residue and the essence of him clung to me not with the saltiness of man, but the exotic, honeyed scent of demon. I'm sure his semen had magical properties, Granny would say so anyway.

I glanced around at this new world. I'd become lazy, a tortured Pandora, roaming naked through Langhousa, my skin fiery in its opalescent glow, my hands in my thatch, fingering my clit until I knew I'd have to sit down and indulge myself. The bed, the floor, the pool, anywhere would do while I waited for him to seduce me, for Bem was ready to indulge me tirelessly in my every whim, perverted dream and fantasy.

My wanton behaviour was worse than whoredom, my body pleasing me in its raw state as I became primal goddess unfettered by garter, cinch or belt, preferring instead the threads of silken devil bondage. I spent hours delicately draped over bed and couch, touching myself and discovering more about this gestating primal scream of demon sex and the pleasures it had unveiled in me. Carelessly I even wandered out undressed into the garden to perhaps gather a mango or admire the flowers, a possessed Eve rolling in the dew-lashed grass.

I shivered in anticipation, the moment I heard his faint susurration or that of his coterie of mischievous attendants. Summoned now by his dark shadow they plagued Anya, who was constantly running into the house and slamming the door. I often found her cowering in the kitchen shaking her head and complaining that the jinn who lived down by the pool at the bottom of the garden had terrorised her again.

She even accused them of stealing her necklace. "Jinn, bad things," she cried, waving her arms about. "Like vapour and sometimes like water, flow everywhere, fly everywhere."

This was true. They were the rustle of leaves in the jasmine bushes, the shadow that flitted around the door, the barely perceptible tingle that made me want to stroke my skin.

Closing my eyes, I enjoyed the cool breeze. What would the ladies of the Chandrapoor Voluntary Society think of me now? I could just hear their voices. 'You're a disgrace to your kind, Emma Spence, you have had a devil's decline in morals.' I laughed and had to clap my hand over my mouth.

Until this moment I hadn't realised how like Granny Rowena I'd become. Some would say Rowena had been depraved. I certainly knew she'd had a liking for young Indian men, one in particular who had tended the temple at Simbali and who she had said was fixated by her and not human at all. Apparently Palak had studied the ways of spirit in his quest to be a priest, and could enter and leave his body and assume the darker coat of some other salacious personality at will. I'd seen him once and he'd seemed very young to me but he had had a glint to his eye and he had moved in the way those touched by the jinn always seemed to move – sinuously and sexy, more creature or elemental than human.

Sometimes, Rowena would be lying on a couch whilst he had massaged her feet. I knew he had lain in her bed but it hadn't seemed to matter. She had said the kind of sex Palak gave her was rather more than the typical white English woman could bear – it was a quest, a quest for delight and melding. This could only be achieved when you threw off the hunger for a quick fuck and ventured into the deeper spirit of sex. Palak and Rowena had giggled together like true lovers. She had said one day I'd know why she became so daring and like a girl, and now I did. It was the hankering to have the sensations mortal man couldn't and didn't want to give, with his roughness and lack of patience, and that bound a woman in so much frustration.

I leaned against the door deep in thought before casting a backward glance at Bem. Lying sprawled on the bed, a smile on his face, he looked similar to any other man in the cocoon of sleep, except he was an Indian god with a halo-like nimbus clinging around him. The nimbus emitting every so often a spark, a blue ember that detached itself, flickered and died.

I walked over to the mirror and, admiring myself, I turned this way and that. My eyes were haunted by my debauched lusts and my normally heavy breasts seemed rounder and fuller, the hennaed nipples even darker and lusher from the constant suckling of his lips. I adored this body much more than I ever did before, and I revelled in the joy it gave me. It was a whore's body and capable of forbidden pleasures. Stretching up on my tiptoes, I touched my skin, groaning with hunger at the masochism burgeoning inside me, tracing the slippery tracks of his kisses and fondling my tender buds and the marks around my wrists. Every day, consuming me continually, he was binding me tighter and tighter with his silken skeins, devilish hands, his cock and mouth.

I wondered at what cost I'd taken an immortal lover. It had driven others insane. Mortals generally lost their minds when they became interwoven in forbidden threads of lust. They became haunted souls, wanderers and hermits or pilgrims, similar to those Stockley shook his head at sorrowfully when we passed them on our way to town. These dispossessed souls were forced to live in eternal meditation, recluses in communities such as Pamlakar, high up in the mountains. Touched by dark magic and demons they were consigned to a life of hell, where a raindrop, a leaf or a spider's web brushing the skin was enough to send their bodies into convulsions. I'd seen an example of such ecstasies myself only the other week. On the roadside, a poor soul had been pinned to the ground by his friends. Little more than a shell, and possessed by jinn magic, he had thrashed out his ecstasy. The man had had no control over his mortal body and had been was unable to function as a human. He had been so blinded by his vision of the other side that the day to day business of caring for his human form had ceased, leaving it a simple shell or perambulatory instrument, a tiresome load in the face of so much eternal bliss. There was nothing to be done except to let it run its course. I had made Stockley pull the car over and I had handed one of the men some rupees. These people were homeless and destitute and at least it would have been enough for the price of a meal and a bed for the night before they had continued their journey.

Twisting my hair around my finger, I wondered what fate awaited me. What had I done? Had I been too greedy and too selfish? Shankar was dead, there was no disputing it, and yet now here he was. Except it wasn't him, was it? Only a manifestation of him. Creeping back to the bed, I sat down, stroking his face and dipping my head to let my lips travel over his skin. I entertained no illusions about him. I knew what he was and what Shankar had become. Shankar's soul was now in the thrall of a dark lord of fire and no ordinary jinni this one, but a patriarch and king of a world of heat and lust. Should I have loved a jinni of the ocean or cosmos I'd probably have been airy like a dust mote, swept deep into the ocean or the bursting centre of a star. As it was, I was a corrupted soul, possessed by a germinating elemental spirit who fed my lusts and who daily became more carnal and salacious.

I couldn't resist it. Wetting my finger I stroked the tip of his penis, gently peeling back the foreskin so I could marvel once again at how human he seemed. I teased it with my nail and watched his cock thicken and weep its beads of juice.

"How naughty, Emma. What a bad woman you've become," I scolded, scooping his ejaculate and smoothing the slick, magical ambrosia over my breasts and inside my legs. And I'd found out there was magic in this unearthly nectar, for it was from the realms of the elemental and it contained the burning power of elemental life that flowed in a roiling river inside me, fuelling me to the heights of passion.

People had noticed the changes in me lately and I was not immune to the comments behind raised hands. After all, my hair was changing colour and becoming even paler and finer, my eyes were brighter, albeit haunted by a sinister light, and my skin possessed an opalescent radiance from the orgasmic glow surrounding me, the orgasm never leaving me completely, but clinging in fine, frosted spider's webs over my skin. Only last week I'd gone to town for some trimming for my dress and Mrs Wilkins had stopped me, her mouth hanging half open in surprise. "Why, Emma, whatever's the matter?"

"I wasn't aware anything was the matter?"

"Oh, it is, look at you, you've always had such wonderful skin, but now, well, tell me what you do? What regime do you follow to make you glow so much?" Her knuckles touched my barely powdered cheek. How could I have told her that Bem's issue smoothed so lovingly on my flesh seemed to be the key to immortal beauty? That, and a diet of salacious, dark sex.

It was laughable that after so many years of futilely pursuing a dream of bliss and burying my head for hours on end in dusty old alchemical and magical sex tracts, I thought couldn't possible exist, now suddenly here it was at last. The answer was in a demon.

I curled my soft, warm body around his aroused one, his penis hard against my leg and temptingly close. Then, I slithered down and began tasting him, seeing if I could wake him by the actions of my tongue and for good measure closing my teeth around him until he opened his eyes, immediately awake, his fingers nestling in my butt.

"Oh, yes."

He took me from behind, sinking his tool deep inside my rear, making dancing movements with his fingers up my spine and, grasping my hair, twisting it out of the way to caress my nape. Stars exploded and my vision was full of spiralling constellations and breathless anticipation, my body resonating, bringing me to a shuddering finale, in tune with his in-and-out thrusting. I laid curled up against him and his long lashes shadowed his cheek as he stroked my skin. Absorbed into his wondrous existence, the moments when I returned to this mortal world were becoming less and less.

"What a tease you are, Emma, you're enough to drive a demon insane."

The fire rose in pulses deep in my womb, and rolling over I turned my attention to his still rigid shaft.

Twisting my hair around his hand, he forced my face down and I gave his phallus a vicious licking before wriggling back up the bed. Thirsty, I'd decided I would show him the extent of my lusts and, spreading my legs either side of his head, I snuggled my crotch above his mouth, resting back on my arms to await the attentions of his tongue. I enjoyed watching his fleshy lips playing, when he peeled back the fragile layers, pinching them all the way up and down, his tongue continuing to work in a burning symphony. Sex was an orgasmic fantasy, a voyage of celestial discovery with Bem and my legs shook and my anklet jingled. In public with my best dress on, these bells invited scandalous gossip. "Here comes the eccentric Emma Spence, with her bells calling the jinn."

Bem raised his head and grinned at me and I sunk my fingers into his lustrous raven-dark hair, drawing his head down so he was forced to suck me harder, to suck out my core.

Chapter Sixteen

"*Mem-saab*, it's Miss Merkel," Anya announced the next morning.

"Merkel," I mumbled sleepily, yawning and unwinding myself from the bed sheets. Why's Merkel here? I rubbed the key around my neck, my gaze flitting to the box on the table, covered by its black cloth. Outside, the sun was shining brightly off leaves still wet from last night's shower.

I remembered now, although it seemed half in a dream. I'd written to Merkel in Madrapor where I knew she'd been helping with the victims of a landslip, explaining to her that I was in trouble and asking if she would she come to help me. It was getting worse, much worse. I was plagued day and night by sexual visions and I was beginning to feel like my body didn't belong to me anymore. I was so blissfully happy, but I knew that I needed to find a solution as to how I could live in two worlds, and Merkel was the only person I could ask.

"Have you asked her in, Anya? Show her to the parlour and take in tea. Tell her I'll be there, the moment I'm dressed."

"Yes, Miss Emma." Anya's stare was reprimanding, but she didn't say anything when she shuffled out of the room.

When I walked barefoot into the parlour, the anklet jingling, Merkel was sitting by the door onto the veranda sipping her tea. She had on a simple blue serge dress and her hair had grown down to her shoulders in a flat curtain that she kept tucking behind her ears.

"I came the moment I could," she explained. "You told me it was urgent, that you were in some kind of spiritual trouble. What is it?" Then her lips compressed into a thin line. "Heaven's above, Emma." Her gaze danced over me. "Have you looked in a mirror lately?" She jumped to her feet and opened her arms so I could run into them. "Daughter of my soul, your feet are filthy, do you never wear any shoes? And you look as white as a ghost." She touched my cheek. "Gracious, perhaps you are a ghost."

I sat down in my favourite rattan chair with my legs curled under me, a queer feeling dancing up my spine like someone trailing their fingers along the keys on a piano keyboard.

"I'm fine, Merkel. In fact, I'm better than fine, but I need to ask your advice." My hands began to move restlessly in my lap. Bem said I had the hands of a whore. My fingers were long and flexible and a constant erotic turn on for him, since they seemed to be constantly engaged in sensual bending and winding like I was recollecting touching something that had given me immense satisfaction.

Merkel took a cigarette out of her cigarette case and, lighting it, she slowly waved the smoke away. "Your letter was so strange. I got it the day I was due to come back. Imagine my surprise when stopping off in Calcutta I bumped into Amelia Fairbright and she said she'd called on you some weeks ago. What she told me cemented what I'd thought. That you were in some kind of spiritual fix."

"Amelia," I said thoughtfully. I had trouble recalling that particular day as my mind fought to reassemble fragments punctuated by fluid moments of sexual tension.

"Yes, she said she wouldn't call again and that you were rude and didn't seem to be in your right mind at all due to a kind of fever. You know what a gossip she is? Well, as a result you're the talk of Chandrapoor. Men still find you intriguing you'll be glad to know, but the women are speculating over you losing your mind and becoming just like your mother. Any day I think they expect to see a white van coming to pick you up and spirit you away to that dreadful place."

I looked up. A brightly plumaged parakeet landing in a tree had unnerved me. "Oh, well, let them speculate. India is changing anyway. Soon things will be different here and Amelia's such an interfering busybody."

Merkel studied me, her glance speculative. "Dear Emma, we've known each other most of our adult lives so why don't you tell me the truth. You've done something just like you said you would, haven't you? I heard a rumour that a woman with striking fair hair was seen going to that devil Bodekar's house in Delhi. To be honest, you were always such a resourceful little thing and I'm hardly surprised you'd try and seek some spiritual solace over Shankar. But dear, that black-hearted demon of all people?" A thin trickle of ash dropped from her cigarette. "My Lord. What did you have Mr Bodekar do? Some kind of conjuration?"

"Yes, I did." I stroked my dress with my finger. "I couldn't live without Shankar and since I'd trapped his soul and I knew it was possible..." My voice trailed off. "Why shouldn't I?"

"But Bodekar, dear? He conjures incredibly dark things using elemental magic, blood and menses, even body odour."

The room was silent except for the ticking of the clock. Merkel examined her hands she seemed to be fortifying herself, ready for what she had to say next. "It's not that I blame you, Emma. I know what a taste of the dark side can do. I deal with it all the time when I take a séance. Grief's a terrible thing and people will go to any length to talk to their loved ones, but black magic, darling?" Her gaze was wistful.

I felt the familiar stirring when I glanced towards the box. A thin shaft of sunlight was playing over it and fingering the keys, I felt compelled to open it right this second.

"Shankar left me the box," I explained. "It's tremendously powerful and of course I had Rowena's book on souls. That was what gave me the idea. Vasi was responsible for doing the last rites and I seized the opportunity. I took my beloved's soul and put it in the jinn box. Naturally..." I poured myself a cup of tea. "The soul was no good to me like that so I went to Mr Bodekar to give it a body and now I have my own genie in a bottle, or as Marion would have put it, a spirit lover."

"Ugh, and how did that beast do it? How did he conjure this thing, because you know it can't really be your lover? All it is, is a coat, a shell, and for heaven's sake the box is a devil prison. How could you be sure there wasn't something dreadfully evil in there?"

"Well, actually, there was an evil soul in there. Well, not exactly evil." I paused, fixing her with my gaze. "Remember that day when I told you what I was going to do? Well, I didn't tell you the whole story. In the box there's an elemental jinni, a sex jinni."

Merkel was wrestling with herself and her inner emotions. She'd become exceedingly pale. "When you put the soul in the box you were bound to know there was a possibility such a thing might possess it?"

"Oh, it did possess it, but you see, Shankar told me he had an affinity with Bem and he was enticed by the demon world. He'd been communicating with Bem Hazari for quite some time. He found his world…how can I put it, seductive."

Merkel leant forward in her chair, shaking her head. "That couldn't possibly be the Bem Hazari, could it? The ancient legendary jinni, the one who wreaked havoc with sex?"

"Yes, the very one."

"Gracious, Emma, he's one of the most powerful spirits of all and you're talking flippantly about possession. You of all people should realise how dangerous that is. I spend half my life repairing souls driven crazy or plunged into mortal hell by superstitions over possession and magic. You and I walk between worlds. We know how strong the forces of good and evil can be, and how alluring that dark side can seem."

"It's not like you think, darling. Bodekar made a fabulous body, I honestly couldn't tell the difference and this, well…it's a beautiful thing, the best thing. I'm sure this was what Shankar in his dark way desired. Merkel, don't be angry, you don't realise how much I love him. I searched all my life for my soulmate never thinking for a minute I'd find him, then when Shankar was snatched away, I didn't know how I'd be able to bear it. What's the good of having this?" I waved my hand at the room. "All this wealth, if you have no love, no direction, if you feel spiritually empty and craving? When you've lost the only man who has the key to your heart?" Leaping to my feet, I came and sat down beside her. "You're the only person who can help me." A tear slid down my cheeks.

"So now you command an elemental devil?"

"Well, not command him. I suppose you'd call me his gaoler," I whispered.

Merkel shivered, casting a glance at the box. "I believe such boxes are the devil's instruments. And what do you think will be the outcome of this? A spirit as evil and manipulative as Bem Hazari will always be looking for a way to escape and you've given it to him. He's a demon, he'll control you. It will become a game of spiritual domination. If anything you will become more confused about the world you belong to than you are already."

I squeezed her hand tightly. "Merkel, I know what I'm doing."

However, Merkel was exceptionally angry and two bright spots of colour marked her cheeks. "You've sold your soul to the devil, you might even be possessed. I understand about demon love, Emma. Enough people have turned to the shadow worlds to fulfil their lust."

"Then I'm possessed. But it's a happy possession." A tear trickled down my cheek and splashed my hand. Surely Merkel would help me because I honestly didn't know what to do. On the one hand I was happy and drowning in lust-filled fantasy, on the other I knew it was impossible to function as a human being in the grip of two worlds.

We seemed to sit silently for ages, the tea turning cold and the sky becoming dark and stormy with the far off rumble of thunder. Suddenly, tapping a long curl of ash off her cigarette she said quietly, "Well, I suppose I ought to do something, you're my oldest friend after all, and I love you."

"Merkel, thank you, you don't know what this means to me."

Merkel shook her head. "I wouldn't get too excited, I don't even know what you want me to do yet, or if I can help."

I was silent for a moment while I fought to formulate the words in my head, then, brushing the tears from my eyes I said, "Merkel, I'm desperately in love but I'm torn in two. I need to find a way to live in both worlds before he steals my mind and leaves me a shell. You see, I can't live in his world and he can't live in mine, but somewhere along the line there has to be a solution and I have to find that solution. If not I'm going to become one of those drifting dispossessed. I've got terrible fears about what happened to Serena. Of course, I've written out my will, but well, in cases of supposed insanity one wonders if it can be overturned and everything sold to pay for my nursing home fees."

"Darling, that's mad, I'm sure it won't come to that, a will's a will." She turned the stub of her cigarette around and around in her fingers.

"I need a spiritual answer, Merkel."

Merkel nodded, touching her lips thoughtfully. "For such a spiritual conundrum, you'd have to go to Pamlakar. You should speak to someone like the

Aamir. The Aamir deals with souls trapped in possession and Pamlakar is a haven for the dispossessed, those who can live in no other place and who seek refuge, and Lord knows there are enough of them." Her gaze softened, then she turned to me and hugged me. "I love you, Emma, and I want to help, but it's impossible to guarantee the Aamir will grant you an audience. However, he was close to my father when Daddy was ambassador and furthermore, he's always been fond of me. I'm going back to the hospital. If you could be ready to leave on Monday you could come with me and I'd take you there."

"You'd do that for me?" I asked.

"Yes, dear." She smoothed my cheek. "I must try and save your soul."

Chapter Seventeen

We set out by train, then it was a long trek across country and up into the mountains with the help of Merkel's *syce* and donkeys. It was a journey Merkel was familiar with because she'd done it so many times before. I had never seen this side of India and I was struck with wonder at the remoteness of it.

When we approached the mountains, the sides of the road became almost impassable due to the steady trickle of pilgrims trekking south, making their way to the religious temples. Every so often the route was marked with shrines where they paused to lay out food and flowers and kneel to say their prayers. Young and old struggled to make this sacred journey to Pamlakar and the path was littered at the side with penitents who believed in the healing energies of the place and would do anything to reach their destination, but had evidently given way under the demands of such an arduous journey. I felt sorry for them because we were on the same mission, to find ourselves or at the very least to find answers to the spiritual questions plaguing us.

One day we passed a woman with her two sons who were fighting, despite their bundles of supplies, to manage their heavy load—a bier on which laid the woman's father, an old man. Their devotion amazed me, since they could hardly manage the bier. Resting every so often, they clambered to their feet, the woman with great fortitude and a brave smile, coaxing them all to yet another mammoth effort to lift the old man and start out once again.

It was much colder due to the altitude and the air was bracing and crystal clear. Each night when the *syce* and servants unpacked the donkeys, a camp was made with the tents set up around a blazing fire. Merkel and I sat before the flickering flames with our shawls around our shoulders, staring at the distant peaks rimed with snow and touched by moonlight. The strange thing was, I felt at home here and for the first time in ages I was happy and full of energy. It was a difficult journey, though, and every evening the *syce* bathed my blistered feet and applied a salve and I rolled into my blankets and was instantly asleep, my hands clasped around the box.

Often I woke in the night and traced the wood, fingering the keys around my neck. I felt like the warder of a prisoner and the guilt washed over me in waves. Bem had not defied me to bring him here. In fact, in the end he had been meek, although of course he'd pleaded and cajoled and even tried to kiss me into submission so I would change my plans. In the end, though, he'd returned to the box and done so in good grace. That didn't change the fact that although I was human, I had a great sensitivity for the spirit world and I felt guilty consigning him to this prison.

Still at the mercy of my own petty fears, for some reason the spiritual atmosphere at Pamlakar was making me see things in a different light and with this came an acceptance and a need to simply be myself. I didn't want to hide anymore. Bem had been right, why not release him? I hugged the box tighter as I thought I heard him lightly tapping against the walls, and he whispered, "Darling, Emma, do you hear me? Darling Emma, talk to me."

A tear rolled down my cheek. Insanity was an insidious thing and it had affected so many of my family. How did you know when you broke that final strand tying you to who you knew you were? When did you know you had descended into a fantastical world of craziness? Well! I knew I wasn't mad. I was determined to beat this, I would find a way. I was madly in love. I'd always adored Shankar and now there was no getting away from the fact I loved Bem. I had to find some kind of higher wisdom to help me to understand a demon's world and to do that I had to grasp my bravery in both hands. That night I fell asleep with my head resting on the box and I dreamt of his tempting demon body sliding beneath the blankets next to me, holding me and caressing me.

The day before we began the final ascent to Pamlakar, we stayed in a village that Merkel knew about. It was a spiritual enclave, a place of special energies frequented by the penitents who for the price of a few rupees could rest their heavy loads and take a while to gather themselves and regain their strength before their final assault on the steep path leading to the holy summits. The village was only a cluster of rudely built homes and we rented one such tiny house, really, little more than a couple of rooms. The amenities were appalling, but it was clean, the lack of comfort more than made up for by the view. My room had two doors leading onto a rickety veranda that clung to the precipitous stony slope and looked straight down below into the gorge with its roaring river. The river descended in a number of cascades from the holy peak and a constant trickle of pilgrims scrambled down the hundreds of steps to the riverside where they bathed in the icy cold waters, washing away their bad karma and hoping to cure illness. Families also brought their ashes here, which after a short ceremony were scattered across the waters.

Despite the altitude the sun was warm and I changed into my cotton shift and twisted my hair in a long plait down my back. I'd carried my box with its special cargo all the way from Chandrapoor, even though Merkel's *syce* had kept trying to convince me he could transport the heavy thing for me. Now sitting on the narrow bed, I stretched my aching limbs and after eating a mango, I began carefully unwrapping the box, lovingly running my fingers over it. It was hard to believe that inside was my captive lover.

Merkel left early the next day to see if she could get an audience with the Aamir and when she eventually came back she looked exhausted. "Well, I talked to the Aamir at last." She yawned, slumping down in a crude chair on the veranda and sipping the tea I'd brewed. "He can be an obstinate old devil and for a while there I thought he'd keep me waiting days."

"Tell me what he said and stop teasing me," I demanded.

"The Aamir said he'll grant us an audience tomorrow but you must be prepared for him, Emma. The Aamir takes his instruction from the spirit world and the answer you're looking for is not assured. He speaks the truth from his heart centre, that powerful centre of spiritual power, and we all know the truth can sometimes be hard to take." She was staring at me pointedly.

That night I couldn't sleep and I was up and dressed at dawn, bubbling with a mingled sense of excitement and dread. I knew that even with the help of the *syce* it would be a steep walk up the mountain and many of the penitents never made it to the top. Then, when we did get to our destination, I had the Aamir to face, and I had to admit the thought of seeing the esteemed holy man filled me with horror. I sat down and began unstrapping my tough walking sandals.

"What are you doing?" Merkel enquired, throwing back her thin blankets and sitting up, stifling a yawn.

"I intend to walk barefoot up the mountain, like the other penitents." I grinned at her. "It'll do me good, I want to do it."

"But you're not a penitent, Emma, and you're not used to it. The rocks will tear your tender feet to shreds. At least let my *syce* carry the box."

"No." I adjusted the straps that I used to carry the box, across my shoulders. "You wouldn't understand. This is something *I have to do*, Merkel."

Clambering up the steep path, the sharp rocks tore at my tender flesh, but I tried not to think about my feet. Thankfully, the stunning panorama diverted my attention. It was spectacular and just like being on top of the world – the snow-capped mountains and passes spreading out around us. Soon we came to a crude crossroads marked by a pile of loose stones where prayer banners snapped in the wind and bells jingled. I placed my hand over my heart, my breath catching in my throat. I could see the vaporous shadows clinging around this holy place and feel the intensity of their spirits and my heart jumped with excitement. Pamlakar was throbbing with the energies of the otherworlds. Here it was as if the veil separating our mortal world from theirs was so thin they were rubbing shoulders. I began to feel I only had to close my eyes and step forward and I'd be able to cross over.

"We have to take the left fork. We're going down that path over there," Merkel said, pointing. "Few people go this way, only those with a special question for the Aamir. Most will continue upwards, heading towards the healing temple." Putting her hand on my shoulder, she directed my attention to the cliff face rising above us, which was peppered with caves. "There's something I ought to say, Emma. The great Aamir is not like other priests, he's more like your friend Vasi. He deals in the dark spirit world not the world of light like the other priests do. It's true they tolerate him as a great man and seer but he was never accepted into the other temples. You see, he was cast out from the priesthood for his ability to talk to dark jinn and dark spirits. That's why he lives in exodus apart from the others, alone in this cave. His is a special vocation, he's an intermediary between dark and light and only he can ordain the lighting of the Holy Jinn Fires at the special jinn shrine."

I shivered, glancing towards the mountain, where I could barely make out the summit and the roof of the small domed temple, the thin string of penitents were heading towards. I realised unlike the Dalai Lama and other great holy men, very little was actually known about the Aamir of Pamlakar and few people spoke about him. Evidently this was why. He was shrouded in some of the same dark mystery Bem was shrouded in. This made my heart beat faster. Surely that meant he would understand me, though. Goodness, I did hope so. I felt more convinced than ever in that moment that I'd done the right thing coming here.

Soon we turned off along another narrow twisting path with a dizzying drop on one side, the path becoming narrower and steeper, our way peppered by tumbled boulders as we headed towards the Aamir's cave, a yawning dark hole in front of which sat an Indian boy dressed in robes.

Merkel turned me to face her, tucking a loose strand of hair behind my ear. "There, you look presentable enough. Now, Emma, the Aamir speaks good English and he's a learned man. If he asks you anything answer honestly, okay?"

"Okay."

Smiling at the boy who had got to his feet, we followed him inside the cave. After the blinding brightness of the sun and the snow-clad slopes, I stood blinking, my eyes taking a moment or two to adjust. Out of the darkness shuffled an old woman with a bowl of water.

Merkel, bowed and said her thanks, then sitting down on a large boulder began unstrapping her sandals. "We must wash our feet and hands, it's so important. In my pack, I've brought jasmine flowers and a flask of wine and of course some dates, to be given as offerings." Merkel raised an eyebrow. "Oh, Emma, don't tell me it slipped your mind?"

I balanced on the rock, cupping the water over my sore, bleeding feet. To be honest I hadn't thought of anything because my mind had been clouded by the traitorous thing I was doing. I dried my feet and, accepting the cup of water the old woman brought us, took time to gather myself and look around. Soon, the boy reappeared and he led us further inside until we lost sight completely of any light from the mouth of the cave. I felt shivers up my spine. Now the only illumination was provided by the odd guttering oil bowl set into a hole in the wall. Every so often smaller caves led off to right or left and my ears were full of strange whispering sounds caused by the wind.

The Aamir was to be found sitting cross-legged in a natural recess in the rock face right at the back of the cave. Surrounded by a huge quantity of food and trinkets piled haphazardly on the floor, he looked just like a king in his counting house sitting on his pile of treasure. It was a mysterious place and I gazed around myself in wonder. Man must have lived here in some form for many centuries because the walls were covered in ancient Sanskrit carvings and niches in the wall were filled with ancient relics.

The Aamir himself, dressed in white robes, was an impressive man. His eyes were closed as if in contemplation and barely a tremor of emotion showed on his placid features. The boy said something to Merkel and she pulled me down gently onto the floor so we were sitting in front of him.

"It's important to wait," she whispered. "The Aamir will talk when he's ready. You see, he's continually in consultation with the spirit world."

I looked at the Aamir. In one respect, with his long white beard, he seemed very old indeed, but his face had hardly a line to spoil the smoothness of his skin, and when he opened his eyes they were exceedingly bright and perceptive and seemed to see right through me. It was only when I unstrapped the box, placing it protectively on my lap, that I saw a flicker of real emotion cross his face.

Leaning forward, the Aamir smiled at Merkel then he stared directly at me. "This is she?"

"Yes, this is Emma, Emma Spence from Chandrapoor."

"Ah, yes, Emma Spence. I remember your grandmother. I met her at a function in Chandrapoor, a fabulous lady." He stroked his beard. "What have you brought me by way of an offering child?"

I had to think quickly. "I think a donation to the temple is good, Aamir."

The Aamir placed his hands together thoughtfully. "One does not usually make such a donation."

"I thought it would be the most useful thing, Aamir."

Merkel sat fighting back an amused smile, with her chin on her hand.

"An ancient jinn box," he exclaimed, staring at the box cradled on my lap. "Come closer, please."

Standing up, I put the box at the Aamir's feet.

Placing his hand on it, he closed his eyes. "Mmm, I thought so, truly powerful. Made by Ravrankar around the date of the Christ. I know this box, it belonged to Nehru Maravar."

"Shankar Maravar was my lover," I said bravely. "When he died he left me the box and told me I might one day have to make the journey to the Holy Fires. As you must know, Aamir, he was the last son of his line."

Looking at me, the Aamir sat back rearranging his robes. "So you have come back to give the box to the Holy Fires."

Merkel shot me a warning glance. "Emma, tell the Aamir the truth."

The Aamir was peering at me and I felt cold all over. How could I tell him what I'd done?

"Emma went to a weaver of black magic in Chandrapoor. Tell him, Emma."

I lowered my gaze. I couldn't look at the Aamir when I explained my story. Afterwards he was silent.

"Come closer, Emma Spence."

I shuffled forwards on my knees and the Aamir placed his hands on my head. Immediately, I felt a curious tingling energy enter my third eye followed by a piercing shaft of light, which seemed to shoot through me, making my whole body vibrate.

"Always mortals want to play with the spirit world since they think they have all the answers to life and death, but it's dangerous to play with shadows. I know better than anyone the powers of these other worlds, Miss Spence, because my life and the lives of many like me are spent in trying to understand them. We live in stillness, meditating and talking to that world. We try to learn from spirit and thus keep strong the tether between man and spirit."

"What are you trying to tell me? These stories of ancient wisdom are not my story, Aamir. How are they meant to help me?"

I thought I saw a flicker of amusement in his eyes.

"Yes they are. They're extremely pertinent to your story, Miss Spence. Special people like you still retain a fragment of memory, a tenuous cord to spirit. You see spirit in everything. In every raindrop and snowflake, and that is a wonderful thing. But also you are subject to great temptations, the temptations of the bliss of spirit for instance, often felt through sex. Shankar Maravar was a very spiritual man, perhaps a weak man, a man drawn a little by darkness. Love, Miss Spence, is an age-old story, studded by passionate acts and emotions and made the stronger by two powerful spirits, it is not entirely of this world."

It was terrifying that the Aamir seemed to be able to see inside my mind and know me so well.

"Miss Spence, look at me." Tipping up my chin, he peered at my face. "What do you truly seek?"

I struggled for words, feeling tears pushing behind my eyes. "I feel torn, Aamir. I feel like I'm possessed by temptations stronger than myself. I want to know how to live in two worlds because I cannot lose my lover again even though I know I did a terrible thing. But how can a mortal girl ever live in two worlds? That is"—I was aware I was groping for words to express myself now—"how can I live as a mortal when I feel such an attraction to the world of my lover, a jinn spirit?"

"Hard choices lay ahead, Miss Spence. I could give you dispensation to visit the eternal fire so that you could send this spirit back to his kingdom. But I caution you that the soul of your lover and the spirit of Bem Hazari are living in symbiosis and now one may not be able to live without the other. However, I will think about your predicament and see if I can find some other solution. I will send for you, Miss Spence."

I wiped the tears from my face with my sleeve as Merkel and I stumbled back down the hill. "That didn't go well did it?" I mumbled. "From the look of disapproval on his face I have the feeling the Aamir thought I was incredibly foolish."

"Fiddlesticks, he liked you immensely and the Aamir is wise enough to know the mistakes humans make. That was a much longer audience than usual. You're lucky if you get the Aamir to talk to you at all. Now you have to wait and see what happens."

Chapter Eighteen

For the first time in ages I felt truly at home. Yes, life at Pamlakar seemed hard with none of the comforts I'd been used to. But for once I felt I could truly be myself without people gazing at me and criticising eccentric Miss Spence. I was spellbound when I conversed with or listened to the pilgrims, and after a day or two I'd become used to the dispossessed souls who wandered from place to place, with vaporous spirit shadows clinging to them. Here, people were aware of just how thin the veil was separating us from our world and that of spirit and that we were all walkers in two worlds. Suddenly it didn't seem so strange being the companion of a demon in a place where people actively chattered to the clinging spectres. It didn't take me long to wonder if maybe I could be of some use and the germ of an idea began to take shape. It seemed the priests were always looking for volunteers and devotees to help with tending the sick who'd made the great journey, offering comfort and providing food.

Merkel was due to leave the next morning. She had to travel back down to the hospital to help with a new outbreak of malaria, but I knew I wouldn't be leaving with her. I wanted to immerse myself in these energies and I had a feeling…a feeling I really could be at peace here.

I sat on the veranda, untying my hair and shaking it free around my shoulders. It was an exceedingly warm morning and the sun was casting its orange glow over the snow-capped mountains.

Rubbing my neck I sighed, and stretching I put my hands behind my neck. Far away I could make out the shrine at Pamlakar, its domed roof glistening in the sun.

Merkel had told me it was an exceptionally special place because inside the modest temple wonderful miracles happened. This holy mountain as distinct from the other taller ones around it, was the true home of the jinn and had been from the dawn of time. In order to go to the temple and visit the fires at the peak you had to have the Aamir's blessing to walk the thousand steps to its summit, and of course, it being the home of the jinn, you could be disappointed in the shrine inside, little more than a hole in the lee of the rocks in which burnt the eternal fire.

I wanted to go to this special place but I knew I needed time and I wasn't quite ready to see the jinn's spiritual meeting point yet—their centre, a place caught between their world and ours where the jinn returned to fire and were reborn from fire. I was hoping for another special audience with the Aamir, when I intended to state my case and beg to be allowed to study under the tutelage of one of the priests. These priests communed with the world of the jinn and I knew their knowledge would open me up and allow me to understand Bem's world better. It was a tall order since few novices—and especially a woman like me—would ever be allowed such a concession. Turning the keys around in my fingers, I pressed them to my lips. Granny Rowena had always said I was a determined woman and I would try to wear the Aamir down. I was sure he felt some empathy with me.

It would be winter soon and I wondered how it would feel being a penitent making that long climb in my bare feet over sharp stones and thick snow.

At that moment, Merkel flung open the door and, coming into the room, rubbed her hands. "Brrr it's cold. I have astonishing news for you, some amazing news, so don't interrupt me, please."

"Tea?" I picked up the small kettle full of the fragrant brew, and without waiting, poured some into a tiny chipped cup.

Merkel sat down in a chair blowing the steam off the top and sipping it greedily. "I have to leave in five minutes. Are you sure you won't change your mind?"

"No, I'm definitely going to stay for a while, come what may."

"I thought so." Her eyes were shining. "Anyway, the Aamir called me at last. He has a habit of leaving things until the last moment, but this time he said he'd had to make some great deliberations." She began searching around in her deep pockets. "An extraordinary thing happened. I can't ever remember it happening before. The Aamir sent you this."

Carefully, unfolding a piece of cloth, she held up a ring with a mysterious dull brown stone in the centre. "The Aamir said for me to tell you, you have a special soul and that he thinks for the first time this ring is meant for a woman. One of Shankar's forebears left it in the safekeeping of the first great Aamir many centuries ago. The Aamir says it has been waiting for centuries for the right person and that person seems to be you. It's a jinn ring, a commanding ring, you use it to summon and control the jinn and he thinks you might need it because one day you will be forced to make a great journey."

"A journey? What kind of journey and where? Did he say?" Shaking my head incredulously, I stared at the ring Merkel had now placed on the table. "And why me? I'm not that important, am I, surely there's someone more deserving?"

Merkel grinned, shaking her head. "Emma, you are deserving. You're a clever and lovely woman. I do think the Aamir was a bit shocked he had to give this to you, a mere woman, though."

I sat down at the table gazing at the ring. I hadn't touched it but I could feel the energy, that wasn't surprising really. Granny Rowena had been a psychometrist and people had often come to her with their rings and bracelets asking her to hold them and do readings for them, and I seemed to have inherited this talent. I had the feeling when I slipped the ring on something would happen and my heart began to beat rapidly.

"You know I've seen rings like these before. Cults and religious sects have them. My mother had a witch's ring something like it and she swore it could command dark forces." Merkel was sucking thoughtfully on her bottom lip. "When he gave it to me my psychic senses picked up that it could be very powerful indeed. Doubtless it's priceless in magical terms. I think with this you'll be able to control Bem, Emma. It will give you control over both worlds. I'm not sure how, but that's for you to find out. Gosh! I can feel it even from here, you know?"

Reaching out, I the sacred object with my fingertip, giving a yelp. "Ouch. It burnt me. How am I meant to wear that?"

"Don't touch the stone, simply slide the ring onto your finger. In time you'll adjust to its power." Merkel pushed back her chair and got to her feet.

"You're not going now, are you?" I squeaked indignantly

"Yes, I must, I'm late and my *syce* is waiting to take me back down the mountain."

"But Merkel!" I threw myself into her arms. "What will I do without you? I'll be all alone here."

Merkel placed her hands on my shoulders. "You won't be alone, Emma, you silly thing. You'll always have your lover, Bem." She gently kissed my cheeks, squeezing my hands before walking towards the door.

I ran after her, catching hold of her arm, hugging her tightly. "How can I ever thank you?"

"Don't be silly, you don't have to."

My mind was spinning out of control. There was so much I wanted to say to her now she was about to leave. "I left a letter with Mr Panjari in Delhi telling him I might not be back to Langhousa for a while. It'll be fine since Anya and Stockley are living there and they'll write to me care of Mr Panjari if they need me. There are one or two things I've decided. I want to become a penitent. I want to earn the right of holy passage to go up to the temple of eternal fire and I want to learn about his world and what made Bem who he is."

Merkel was staring at me intently. "Yes, yes I think that's the best thing. The Aamir likes you, Emma. He was touched by your devotion. He seems to think if a soul can love so much she risks losing her sanity, it must be great love indeed. Be at the Aamir's cave tomorrow morning, he expects you there, he wants to talk to you. You know you're going to be fine, don't you, Emma? And I'll be back to see you in the spring when I'll see you again, unless, that is…" Pausing for a moment, she turned around on the step. "Unless you've already departed on your great adventure."

A cold shiver ran up my spine, a feeling of presentiment, a sense that in some great way my life was about to change.

"Do you know something, Emma?"

"What's that?"

"I rather envy you having the love of a jinni demon."

Epilogue

I'd released him from the box and I was never going to put him back inside, because now I had the ring. Bem came up behind me and placed his hands over my eyes before playfully kissing my neck. He was wearing a thin robe of glowing purple fabric, and in the centre of his forehead was the mark of his caste, that I'd painted there for him with saffron. Something had altered between us. Maybe it was the potency of this place, perhaps it was the words of the Aamir, but I loved him more than ever and so much I now felt a part of him. Well, they said miracles happened at Pamlakar.

He turned me around and, stroking my cheeks, kissed me gently on the lips, leading me over to the window so we could look out. It was early evening and a glorious sunset stained the white peaks, licking them with fingers of orange fire. Drawing me back he hugged me to him and I felt his cock pressing against my thigh, filling me with delicious yearning. On the path outside the window some penitents were sitting, enjoying the explosive evening display. A woman cradled her baby, feeding it rice from her fingers and from over her shoulders gazed the gauzy face of her spirit companion, so clear now I could see every detail of his youthful face. They turned around and looked at us, sensing Bem's presence and the woman bowed her head in deference to my jinn lord.

"Emma," he whispered. "These people see me as I really am and I truly feel I've come home. I'm so happy, my darling." He walked me backwards, pushing me down on the crude bed, then, kneeling between my legs he lifted my rough cotton dress before sliding his hand up the inside of my thigh. I shuddered with convulsions of delight, his finger crooked within my warm folds began circling and rubbing, raising the fire inside me. In moments I was a sweet rushing river.

"I never thought I'd admit it, but you did the right thing bringing us here, Emma. I feel powerful, driven by a new purpose, and shall I tell you something else?" He was gazing down at me teasingly. "I love you more like this, than I ever loved you in your sexy dresses and pearl necklace."

Giggling, I caressed him, coaxing my hands under his loose robes to run my hands down his beautiful arched spine, savouring his burning jinn skin before kissing his fingers. I slid each one in my mouth.

"This is most definitely made for you, I think." Bem stopped me. He was holding up the jinn ring and where it had brushed his hand it had made a mark like a small brand in his spirit flesh.

"Oh Bem, it burnt you." I licked the wound, felt him shudder with demon lust.

"Yes, but it's a fine pain, it's the pain of belonging to you, my mistress, and not that damn box. I know which I prefer. I am your servant."

I felt an inner sense of triumph and my heart soared at these words. Twining my fingers through his thick hair, I pulled his face closer, tracing around his dark, smoky eyes. "I love you, Bem. No, love is a feeble word. I adore you."

"Are you happy, Emma?"

I nodded, my heart flooding with emotion. "Yes, for the first time ever, I think I can truly say I am."

"Our story is about to be written, do you know that? It hasn't really started." There was a depth in his eyes I had never seen before, a new purpose, and it wasn't just lust.

"Yes, I know. I must stay here a while, Bem. There are things I need to learn about your world that even you can't teach me. I'm going to work amongst these people and discover that inner kingdom of yours and find out about it. This is the only way I can preserve my sanity."

Gripping my chin, he looked into my face, his own radiant with the power of the other world. Then pushing me back hard onto the bed he drew his robes over his head so he was naked, and proceeded to open my legs so he could slither gently inside me. I had no resistance because I belonged to him and him to me. I began gyrating my hips. I could feel the warm fires starting, a slick slow burn at the base of my spine increasing in intensity. Then I was melting, melting once more into that place of dark desire, becoming like molten lava as, pumping and churning, he moved remorselessly inside me.

"There's a place, remember I mentioned it before? The place of Ravrankar where the great magic exists that made my prison and may also be able to free me from it. Darling, I'm happy to be your servant but I dream of the day when that box is no longer my dark cell." Bem rolled my hennaed nipples between his fingers. "I think I might know exactly where it is. It's in Africa many miles away, a place of hot burning jinn sun. The only trouble is it's an arduous journey across sea and desert and..." He winked at me and a slow smile crept over his lips. "I may have to beg the favours of my mistress to carry me there. The time is not yet right for that journey but soon it will be. I'll make you love me so fiercely you'll do anything for me, Emma. One day I will be free."

"How could you ever make me love you more than I do now?" I sighed.

Bem slipped the ring onto my marriage finger and, raising my hand, he kissed it. "Love of my soul, this burning is pleasure." He whispered, "Control me, I belong to you eternally."

About the Author

Alcamia grew up around books and her earliest memory was browsing through dusty bookshops with her father. She started writing for fun when she was a child and loved escaping into imaginary worlds. Alcamia has had a varied career life both in the arts, media and alternative healing and medicine but always had the dream of being a writer, something she's been able to put into practice over the last few years. She started by writing pure romance but says her writing really came alive when she studied Anais Nin and began to put some hot passion and erotica into her stories. An avid science fiction and fantasy buff she also loves exploring all aspects of the paranormal and sciences and hopes that her work will always be fresh and thought provoking and give the reader something to think about.

As she says, 'there's nothing I won't tackle and if I come up with a simple idea for a story whether it's mainstream, gay, lesbian or fantasy - I'll have a crack at it. I like to be continually writing and active.' If asked if she has a first love with story telling - it always has to be a story with a strong and passionate romance as its basis. She also likes her characters to be strong and a bit different and able to accept their faults and use them. She loves giving talks about books and magic, is an ardent lover of nature and cats and enjoys ballet, Victorian costume, collecting books and travelling. She invites you the reader to take a little journey with her through her stories and hopes you enjoy them.

Alcamia Payne loves to hear from readers. You can find her contact information, website details and author profile page at http://www.total-e-bound.com.

Total-E-Bound Publishing

www.total-e-bound.com

Take a look at our exciting range of literagasmic™
erotic romance titles and discover pure quality
at Total-E-Bound.